TIBETAN SECRETS

THE ORIGIN SCROLL, BOOK 1

THE MAXWELL BARNES ADVENTURE THRILLER SERIES

BOOK 4

CRAIG A. HART

PROLOGUE

Tibet, Himalayan Mountain Range, 1939

"This is Apex calling Ultra. Do you read me?"

The heavily bundled man crouched over the radio that sat atop a large wooden supply crate, his lined and grizzled face glowing in the yellow light from the flickering oil lamp that sat on the cave floor a couple of feet away. The rough walls of the cave rose up and inward, with the concave ceiling holding up the untold weight of the mountain peak overhead.

The man adjusted the dials on the radio as he listened intently to the static crackling from the speaker. His breath misted in the frigid air, and he shivered involuntarily, pulling his fur-lined coat tighter around himself. He was no stranger to harsh conditions, having visited some of the world's most inhospitable locations on His Majesty's service, but this mission was beginning to wear on his nerves and break down the vaunted British stiff upper lip.

"This is Apex calling Ultra. Do you read me?"

He had been sending this same message for an hour, but had received no reply. This was unusual, for Ultra—the codename for British intelligence—was known for placing a premium on both promptness and consistency. Every other scheduled check-in had gone as planned, the report sent and acknowledged. But this time was different.

And now he actually had something worth reporting. On his last outing before the storm, he had found something—the thing he'd been sent to investigate. Now he just needed to plan his extraction from this increasingly dangerous region, and he could return home. He cast a single glance at the inscribed wooden box that rested on a folded piece of fox fur. He smiled and then turned back to the radio.

"This is Apex calling Ultra. Do you read me?"

Again, no reply.

The man sat back on his heels and rubbed his bare hands. He'd been forced to remove his woolen mittens to work the radio's controls, and now his fingers were going numb with cold. The storm blowing outside had raged for days—although it seemed like weeks—and he suspected it had something to do with his inability to raise Ultra.

Two days ago, the storm had settled briefly, and he had attempted to make his way down the mountain, abandoning the radio and his supplies. There was not much left anyway, including the dwindling supply of petrol for the generator that powered the radio.

He had not gone far before something—some creature—had forced him to return to his camp in the cave. And now, the storm had returned with full force.

He leaned forward and once more flipped the transmission switch.

"This is Apex calling Ultra. Do—oh, damn it," he broke off and rocked back again. "Well, Reed—you may be about to meet your maker. After all the tomfoolery you've been up to over the years, you're going to die in a cave high in the Himalayas. Not as romantic as it sounds, eh, old chap?"

Jameson Reed had entered the Secret Intelligence Service (SIS) in the late 1920s, during a period of relatively low activity, but had consistently found himself dropped into various hotspots in the British Empire to gather intel and perform other covert operations. From the dusty streets of Cairo to the bustling markets of Singapore, Reed had always been at the forefront of British intelligence gathering. Now that the world was teetering on the brink of global conflict, he was busier than ever. Thus it was that he found himself high in the Himalayas, on an espionage mission against the rising sun of imperialistic Japan.

"But first, I will do my duty and file the report, whether it is being received or not," he muttered. "Then a final cup of tea, followed by whatever Fate has in store." He settled into a more comfortable position and cleared his throat. Then he flipped the transmit switch with his forefinger , wrapped his hands around the microphone, and began:

"Ultra, this is Apex. I don't know if you read me, but this is my filed report of March 29, 1939." Reed cleared his throat again.

"I am alone, and the storm has been raging for days. My Sherpa guide disappeared just before the storm, and I have not seen him since. Two days ago, I thought I might be able to make it down from the mountain during a brief respite from the storm. But some ... thing, forced me back into this cave. A lion, maybe ... or a bear, but I don't think so. Something much bigger, something fiercer, something ... smarter.

"I was forced to retreat back to the cave, where I remained still and quiet, using ash from the fire to disguise my scent. Whatever it was, it finally went away, but by then the storm had returned with all its fury, and I could not leave the shelter. That was the last time I attempted to descend."

Reed was standing now, holding the microphone, concentrating on the report.

"New snow has stopped falling, but the wind still blows so fiercely that it is impossible to see more than a foot or two ahead of you. Without my guide, I would undoubtedly fall into a crevasse or tumble down an incline. If I were to injure myself on the descent, that would be the end of it. I am still hopeful that the storm will settle in time, but I fear that when it does ... the creature will return."

Reed paused, mouth slightly open. He thought he had heard something outside the cave, but as he listened, nothing more could be heard. Even the howling wind seemed to have abated.

"But perhaps the wind is settling now. I will look from the mouth of the cave."

He set the microphone atop the wooden crate that held the radio and turned to walk toward the mouth of the cave.

As he approached, he noticed the heavy blanket he'd affixed at the entrance was blowing less crazily, and the noise from the wind was definitely lessening. Pulling the blanket aside, he peered into the bleak world outside to discover that, indeed, the storm had quieted.

The comfort this realization afforded, however, was quickly vanquished as a new sound cut through the snowy, mountain air—a wailing cry that reverberated through the peaks. Initially, it began as a growl that seemed to originate from hell itself, but as it intensified, the pitch rose, and a feeling of malevolence rose with it.

Reed swore and let the blanket fall.

It was back.

It was close.

And it was coming closer.

He ran for the radio, hoping to complete his transmission. He couldn't die yet—he had yet to send the most important part of the report.

Something huge crashed through the cave's opening, ripped the blanket from its moorings.

Reed heard someone screaming and vaguely realized it was himself.

He was not the type to panic, but what he saw was so overwhelmingly terrifying that his already-weakened resolve crumbled entirely ...

And he screamed.

1

MAXWELL BARNES LAY IN BED IN A HOTEL IN NEW YORK CITY. The alarm clock had been going for 10 minutes straight and somebody was banging on the wall in the next room.

"Turn that thing off," a muffled voice said.

Max knew that voice. It was his best friend from childhood, Axel Morales, and the big man had a voice to match the size of his body.

Max rolled over and compelled his sleepy eyes to open. Immediately, he regretted it as someone—a very rude someone—had opened the blinds in his room, and the morning sun was streaming in like Gabriel's flaming sword. He forced his scorching eyeballs to remain open and looked toward the clock.

The alarm was merciless.

Finally, Max reached out and smacked the top of the machine, forcing it to quiet its earthly wailing.

"Thank you," the muffled voice said.

"You're welcome," Max responded loudly, his voice sounding like broken glass being ground by a wood chipper. The clock now silently displayed the hateful time of seven a.m.

Max normally did not mind early rising. In fact, as an archaeologist who traveled the world searching for unusual artifacts in oft-dangerous locations, he was used to being up at all hours of the day or night. But he and his two friends, Axel Morales and Isabel María García, had spent a late night into the early morning, celebrating. Max could not remember *what* they had been celebrating, but it must have been something worthy because many beers had been consumed.

And now, he was paying for it.

He was tempted to give the clock another smack, this time hopefully destroying the horrible, sadistic device. But he restrained himself, especially since this was not his room and he didn't feel like getting an extra charge on the hotel bill. He forced himself to a sitting position, stretching broadly, reaching his arms toward the ceiling, and uttering an unearthly groan. His muscles screamed in protest at being extended to such lengths, but that was just too bad. If he had to get moving, then his body would have to get moving as well.

Something triggered in his brain, and a surge of adrenaline rushed through him.

Oh crap, he thought, reaching for his tickets. He checked the arrival time and saw that they were indeed on the verge of missing their flight. He jumped out of bed, his heart thrumming to new heights. "Axel! We overslept, we're gonna miss our plane," he shouted, pounding so hard that plaster started to fall down in between the walls.

There was a moment of silence, and then a growled, rumbling curse muffled from the other room. He heard the bed squeak as Axel rolled his massive body off the mattress, and then a thud as two giant feet hit the floor. Max couldn't restrain a smile as he stood and listened to the flurry of activity taking place.

"Don't hurt yourself," he yelled, and then began gathering his own items, packing his overnight bag, running a toothbrush over his teeth, and throwing on clothes. He wet his hand and ran the damp fingers through his mussed, brown hair, trying to tame the worst of the bed-head.

He made a second check of the room just to make sure he wasn't forgetting anything important, then tossed the bags over his shoulder and headed for the door. He and Axel arrived at the hotel hallway at the same moment, looking at each other with wide, frantic eyes, and then headed down for the lobby at top speed.

"Elevator?" Axel asked.

"Not a freaking chance."

Together, they clattered down the stairs, going down three floors, and then burst out into the lobby, like two bulls exiting the rodeo gate. They stopped upon entering the lobby, only to find themselves surrounded by a couple of dozen other patrons currently enjoying a complementary continental breakfast. Out of breath from the frantic rush down multiple flights of steps, they stood, chests heaving, breath wheezing, and offered sheepish and apologetic smiles to the surrounding diners.

"Lo siento," came a silky voice from across the room.

The two men looked up to see Isabel approaching. She was shaking her head and looked like a longsuffering nanny about to admonish two very naughty boys.

"They always act this way," she said, addressing the diners in the room. "They do not know any better. I think both of them were raised in a cowhouse."

A ripple of laughter wafted across the room, and Max's face reddened.

"First of all," he said, "it's not a 'cowhouse,' it's a barn. And second, I think you enjoy humiliating us just a little too much."

Isabel smiled, her plump lips revealing sparkling white teeth. Max could tell she was not in the least apologetic. "I could have done much worse," she said. "You should have heard what I decided *not* to say."

"No thanks," Max said. "By the way, you look like you've been up for a while."

"Why didn't you come and wake us?" Axel asked.

"It is not my job to make sure two grown men can get to their appointment on time," Isabel said curtly. "Besides, I was having mimosa at hotel bar and could not be bothered."

"Wait a minute, you're taking the same flight as we are," Axel said. "What do you mean, you couldn't be bothered?"

"There are other flights," Isabel said reasonably.

Max was still out of breath. He leaned over, placing his hands on his thighs, and gathered his wits. He had to admit Isabel had a point. This was not the only flight leaving New York, after all, and if they missed this one, there would be another. Losing that money would be a shame, but not the end of the world.

"You are ready to eat?" Isabel asked.

"We still have a chance to make the flight," Max said.

Isabel shrugged. "Very well, but I do not want to hear any whining about how hungry you are. One hour from now."

"Don't worry about that," Axel said. "Let's just get to the airport and we can think about food later. Yeah, we could catch another flight, but I really don't want to spend any more time messing around with this than I have to. You know how much I hate airports and airplanes."

The memory of an airport explosion sobered Max quickly. He remembered sitting in a bar in Guatemala and watching television as an explosion on the landing strip came across the news. He thought for sure his best friend had died. Fortunately, Axel had escaped tragedy, but the experience had affected both men deeply.

"Let's go catch a cab," Max said, shaking off the unpleasant memory. "The sooner we get this day underway, the better. It's been kind of a rough start."

~

THE AIRBUS350 LIFTED off the runway at LaGuardia Airport. Max was pressed back into his seat by the upward force, which increased as the plane rose into a clear sky above the factory buildings and brownstones of Queens. As the plane crossed into Newark, New Jersey, it banked over the Hudson River, marred by an industrial port on the western shore.

The towers of Manhattan pressed up from behind the Statue of Liberty like a dark mass.

The flight to Shanghai Pudong International Airport would take around fourteen hours, followed by a connection flight to Lhasa, Nepal, if they were lucky enough to have their permissions honored. Lhasa was located in the Tibet Autonomous Region of China, with limited access and special permit requirements for travelers.

Max was eager for the seatbelt light to go off so he could relax and remove his laptop from its case. He had some work he wanted to do, some research that had been nagging at him ever since he first encountered it several weeks ago. Since then, it had been a never-ending quest for funding and diplomatic clearances.

At last, the Airbus reached its cruising altitude, and the seatbelt light pinged off. A flight attendant made her way down the aisle, stopping at every seat to offer passengers a limited selection of drinks and snacks. Max thought about some of the commercials or print advertisements he'd seen for flights back in the 1950s or 60s. What a time to fly that would have been!

He reached down and pulled his laptop from the case, flipping up the top and waiting until the computer came to life. Using the trackpad, he navigated to a folder on the desktop titled "Himalayas."

Even as he double-clicked the folder to open it, a thrill of excitement charged through his body. This could be the expedition of a lifetime, he knew, and he couldn't wait to get started.

Suddenly, he felt someone kicking the rear of his seat.

He thought for sure it was Isabel causing mischief, but then he saw the back of her head several rows ahead of him. Taking a quick glance over his shoulder, he saw a grubby little redheaded boy grinning at him. The kid had a flat-brimmed hat worn sideways and, as he grinned, Max could see the kid needed braces but had not received them. There was a smidge of something dark on the side of the kid's mouth, presumably chocolate. And the kid appeared to have been eating a lot of unhealthy items his entire life.

"Stop kicking my seat," Max demanded.

The kid kept grinning and kicked again.

Max sighed, swallowed his anger, and turned around resolutely. He was not going to let this little brat ruin his trip, and he had too much to do to spend any more time babysitting.

The folder had opened, and Max looked at the screen. Various icons showed a preview of the file contents: photographs, maps, and text documents. This was all the information Max had been able to gather concerning their current mission. As he looked at it, he had to admit it wasn't as much as he would have liked, considering the amount of money and hassle he and the others had already endured just to make it to this flight. He had to wonder if some of the obstacles thrown up by various individuals and institutions had anything to do with the ultimate goal. A common excuse to refuse funding or unroll spools of red tape had been that the entire expedition would be a waste of time and resources. But Max had wondered from the very beginning if those same entities who were causing him problems simply did not want them to succeed.

Something hit the back of the seat again, and Max swallowed his fury. He was two seconds away from jumping up, dragging the kid down the aisle, opening the emergency hatch, and throwing him out.

"Do you mind?" he asked, turning once more, plastering on the fakest smile in recorded history.

This time when he turned around, he noticed a red-haired woman sitting next to the child. She looked as ill-tempered as the kid, and Max did not hold great hope that appealing to her would serve any good purpose. However, he was an adult, and therefore had to try.

"Ma'am, would you please ask your kid to stop kicking my seat?" Max tried very hard to insert a bit of warmth into his smile. "I really have some work I need to get done, and being interrupted by having something forcefully driven into my back is not conducive to accomplishing that goal."

"Sir, my son isn't doing anything wrong. Please turn around and mind your own business like the rest of us who have paid for a ticket," she said.

If you kill her, you'll spend the rest of your life in jail, Paranoia said.

"I'm not sure I care," Max said, annoyed the familiar inner monologue had chosen this moment to insert itself.

"Excuse me?" the woman shrieked.

Everyone in the general vicinity looked toward them, and Max wanted to sink through the floor, no matter that sinking through the floor would send him hurtling to the earth 35,000 feet below. But that didn't matter. In fact, Max thought he might actually prefer it at this point.

"Something wrong here?" a deep, growling voice asked.

Max looked up to see Axel standing there, his head nearly brushing the top of the airliner's ceiling.

The woman gawked at Axel, and her eyes growing wide. That was a common reaction when people first saw Axel Morales. He was one of the biggest people Max had ever seen. And he was constantly happy his friend was on his side.

"What business is it of yours?" the woman asked, not quite ready to surrender even though her surliness had cooled by several hundred degrees.

"This is a friend of mine," Axel said, pointing at Max. "That's not something I normally admit to strangers, but in this case, I think it is necessary. You see, we are on the trail of a dangerous criminal, someone who particularly likes to kidnap little boys with red hair. Max, here, is tasked with doing the research before we arrive at the criminal's reported location. If you keep kicking the back of the seat, he won't be able to do his preparation, and our suspect will probably escape. Now, do you want that on your conscience?"

"Good heavens, no," the woman gasped, reaching over to grab her child in a tight embrace.

"Good," Axel said. "Then perhaps we can consider this business closed."

Without another word, Axel turned and walked back to his own seat—or rather his own row, since he was too big for a single seat.

Max wanted desperately to dunk on the woman, but he was smart enough to take a win when it presented itself. So, he simply turned around and returned to his laptop.

2

The Airbus descended toward the runway at Shanghai Pudong International Airport, its engines roaring as it neared the tarmac. As the wheels touched down, there was a loud thump and the sound of screeching tires. There was a jolt as the landing gear made contact with the ground, and then a smooth sensation as the plane slowed down and taxied to the gate.

Max held tight to his carry-on, which also contained his laptop. He had always been the type to travel as lightly as possible, especially for someone who spent a great deal of their traveling days in inaccessible locations. After what seemed like an extremely long time, given they had just been flying fourteen straight hours, the Airbus pulled up to the disembarkation tube and passengers prepared to exit.

Gripping his carry-on with both hands, Max looked for his friends. Naturally, Axel was much easier to spot than

Isabel, but eventually he saw them both and met up on the fringe of the bustling center aisle.

Axel spoke first. "You guys wanna get off now, or wait till it calms down a bit?"

"Let's get out of here now," Max said. "I'm ready to find a hotel and catch a rest before we begin the more exciting part of our adventure."

"Sí," Isabel said. "This is the longest flight I have ever been on, and I do not wish to repeat it."

Max grimaced. "Well, I'm sorry to say we're going to do this again on the way home."

"Then I think I will just stay in Tibet," Isabel purred, causing Max's stomach to twist into a pleasant knot.

He wanted to say, "you're not staying anywhere I can't stay also," but he held back, aware their relationship had not yet reached a level of intimacy that would allow for such a statement without it coming across as a joke. However, his feelings for Isabel were genuine, and he was most definitely not joking.

Since their first meeting in La Libertad, Guatemala, his affection for the dark-haired woman had grown steadily. Though it felt like it had been an eternity since they met, in reality, it was not that long ago. The time they'd spent together had been filled with danger, excitement, and adventure, packing a lifetime into a relatively short period. The intensity of their experiences together had deepened the connection, and he could not imagine his life without her.

Max frowned. That last thought had sounded disturbingly like proposal material, and he certainly was not ready to do anything of that nature. Still, he could not deny that losing Isabel would leave a sizable hole in his life. He'd grown used to having her around.

Axel confidently strode down the aisle of the aircraft, his imposing physical presence effortlessly parting the mass of people. Axel had many good qualities, but his ability to command a room and clear a crowd was one of the most impressive, in Max's opinion, and it was particularly useful in chaotic situations like this.

At last, they debouched into the open area of the airport, which was just as busy as the interior of the Airbus had been. The terminal was a bustling hub of activity. Passengers from all over the world rushed through, hurrying to catch their flights or meet loved ones. The sound of various languages filled the air, and the duty-free shops and food courts were crowded with travelers looking for last-minute souvenirs or a bite to eat.

"I really need to get away from these crowds," Max said, his voice tight with tension. "My too-much-social-interaction alarm is going off at full volume."

"I didn't realize you were so antisocial," Axel said, grinning. "But I hear you. Those kinds of flights really take it out of you. Let's get to the hotel, order some food, and watch a little television. Then, after we rest or sleep a bit, you can give us a debriefing from the information you went over on the plane."

"Honestly, you know quite a bit of it," Max said."I learned a few things, but nothing revolutionary. But, yes, we'll go over it."

"Er ... did you learn anything new?" Axel asked.

"Enough to get started, yes. Now, come on—hungry and tired, remember?"

The trio moved through the terminal, at last exiting at the front of the building. To their dismay, it was equally chaotic outside. Taxis, buses, and private cars swarmed the airport's circular drive, each driver honking their horn to attract passengers. The air was thick with exhaust fumes, and revving engines combined to create a discordant roar of sound.

Max groaned and looked pleadingly up into a sky hazy with pollution. "I hate this."

Once more, Axel demonstrated his usefulness by stepping forward and emitting a piercing whistle that somehow cut through the racket. A taxi screeched to the curb just in front of them.

"I take you drive?" the Chinese driver asked.

"Yes!" Max said, rushing toward the vehicle.

The driver jumped out and opened the trunk, waited while his new fares dropped in their bags, and then ran back to the driver's seat. He hopped inside, yelling, "Get in, we go!"

They all climbed into the taxi, which appeared to have seen much better days, with Max sitting in the front passenger seat with his laptop case carried cross-body-style.

"Take us to the nearest hotel that won't give us a disease," he said.

The driver grinned, showing off several missing teeth, and then sent the taxi hurtling into traffic.

"Forget diseases!" Max barked. "Just get us there alive!"

"You 'live,'" the driver said, still grinning like a loon. "You very 'live.'"

The taxi hurtled through the bustling streets of Shanghai, with Max gripping the door handle tightly, expecting at any moment to collide with an oncoming vehicle or careen off the road in a fiery inferno of twisted metal. The driver seemed unfazed by the chaos and navigated the crowded streets with ease. Isabel rolled down her window, and the wind rushed in, whipping her long, dark hair. She appeared to relish the thrill of the ride, her eyes sparkling with excitement.

The lights of the city flew by in a blur, and the sound of honking cars and chatter of the street vendors filled the air. Isabel's laughter could be heard over the din as she leaned out the window, taking in the sights and sounds of the vibrant city.

"Are you actually having fun?" Max asked.

"I have never been on this side of the world," Isabel said, pulling her head back inside the taxi. "It is very exciting for me. How about you?"

"Not yet," Max said. "But hopefully, things will improve once we get to the hotel. I think I'm getting a little hangry."

They rode on wordlessly for a few more minutes, and Max began to have questions about where they were headed. They had passed several decent looking hotels, including some with names he recognized, like Courtyard by Marriott, but the driver had chosen to pass all of these by.

"Where are we going?" Max asked the driver.

"You be very happy with where I take you," the driver insisted. "You will enjoy ride."

"I'd rather just know where we were going," Max said.

"You be very happy," the driver repeated.

Max was too tired to argue, so he sat back and closed his eyes. He tried his best to relax, but he just couldn't get there.

Finally, the taxi came to a crawl, and Max opened his eyes, taking in his surroundings. The vehicle made a sharp turn into a dimly lit parking garage, the bright sunlight giving way to ominous shadows, and Max blinked as his eyes adjusted to the gloom. The air was thick with the stench of exhaust, and the sound of the tires on the concrete floors echoed throughout.

"This does not look like a hotel," Axel said. "What game are you playing, cabbie?"

"I do not know this word 'cabbie,'" the driver said. He stomped on the accelerator again and began flying around the turns in the parking garage, climbing higher and higher.

"Stop this car right now!" Axel demanded, leaning forward.

Max tightened his grip on the door handle even more, preparing to leap out if necessary. Then the taxi came to a sliding, screeching, grinding halt. Max looked ahead ... and his blood ran cold.

There were two black cars, and in front of the cars stood three men in long, dark coats.

"I think we might be in trouble, partners," Max said.

Axel snorted. "What gave you that idea? The fact we appear to be driving onto a movie set, or the fact all of those men just pulled out weapons?"

Max looked again and saw Axel was correct. Every one of the men had indeed pulled out a weapon. Scary weapons. Automatic-type weapons.

"Okay, who are you?" Max demanded of the driver.

"I am just driver," the cabbie insisted. "I know nothing. I only deliver and get paid."

"Oh, of course you got paid," Max said disdainfully. "You're a regular Judas Benedict Quisling."

The driver appeared confused but kept on smiling.

The men were now walking forward, their weapons at the ready.

"You all get out now," the driver said. He was still smiling.

"No, thanks," Max said.

"You get out." Finally, the driver's smile wavered.

One of the armed men had reached the taxi and was violently shaking Isabel's door handle. Isabel had locked it in time, but her window was still rolled down, and the man thrust the muzzle of his automatic weapon through it, so close it was almost touching Isabel's forehead. The act of aggression sent a wave of anger through Max, and his chest turned heavy with burning rage. Instinctively, he wanted to jump to Isabel's defense and protect her from harm, but he knew such an impulsive move would be futile and likely lead to their deaths.

For her part, Isabel remained at least outwardly calm, fixing the gunman with a cold stare from her dark eyes.

Max studied this first man closely, taking in his imposing figure. He was taller than the average Chinese man, with a broad face and thick, furrowed brows that cast a shadow over his eyes, which gleamed with a sinister light. When he sneered at Isabel, revealing his strong, prominent teeth, it sent a chill down Max's spine. The man's presence was menacing, exuding a palpable sense of danger. His smirk was not one of amusement, but rather a display of malice and aggression.

"All of you get out of the car," he said, demonstrating very good English.

No one moved, except for the taxi driver, who was clearly becoming increasingly nervous.

"You pay me money?" the driver said, craning his neck to look at the gunman.

"You'll get your money," the man ground out from the corner of his mouth, not even bothering to look at the driver.

"Perhaps you could tell us what this is all about," Axel said.

Max was impressed at the calm demeanor of his friend, who was known to become quite angry when held at gunpoint. It was one of his least favorite things.

"We can talk when all of you exit the car," the gunman said. "If you refuse, we will simply turn this car into a pin cushion along with all of you inside it."

The taxi driver emitted a low moaning sound, and gripped the steering wheel, his knuckles white with fear.

"Oh, shut up," the gunman said, finally shooting him a glance. "We'll let you leave first before we open fire."

"But my car!" the taxi driver said. "You no shoot up my car!"

Axel looked at Max and Isabel in turn, then said calmly

and quietly, "I don't think we have much choice, guys. I think we do what they say."

As much as Max hated to admit it, Axel was right. They had no choice. They could either die here, in the car, or exit the car and see what these men wanted. They certainly didn't *look* friendly, but sometimes one simply had to let a situation unfold.

Together, the trio unlocked their doors and climbed out of the taxi with a sense of intense trepidation. Max, Axel and Isabel all exchanged a glance, each of them silently acknowledging the eerie atmosphere. The concrete floor was stained and cracked, and the air was thick with the smell of gasoline and car exhaust.

Before they even had a chance to slam the doors shut, the cabbie stomped on the gas and screeched away through the parking garage, the shrieking of tires echoing loudly through the large concrete structure. Max jumped back quickly to avoid his feet getting run over and watched the taxi speed off, shaking his head in disbelief.

"That guy definitely needs a driver's education course," he muttered.

The nearest gunman, the one who had pointed a weapon in Isabel's face, moved over to stand directly in front of the three explorers, and his two partners walked up to join him. One, a shorter fellow with thinning black hair, glasses, and a sparse moustache, stepped one pace ahead of the others.

Must be the leader, Max thought. *Doesn't look like much.*

Hope swirled in his mind. Perhaps these men were

merely government types wanting to flex a little muscle but intending no real harm.

We all just need to stay calm.

The short man stuck his weapon out of sight into his long coat and surveyed them slowly. His eyes appeared large and frog-like behind thick glasses. At last, he spoke:

"Do the three of you have your papers in order?"

"What is this, East Germany?" Axel grumbled.

Max started to respond in kind, but remained calm as he began to reach for his bag, which contained the papers ... before realizing all their luggage was still in the trunk of the departed taxi.

"Is there a problem?" the short man asked.

"Yeah, your little informant dude just drove off with all of our things," Max said, "except my laptop bag."

Beside him, Isabel let out a loud groan.

"That is most unfortunate," the man said. "It would appear we are going to have to take a trip downtown." He gestured toward the long black cars.

"Is that really necessary?" Max asked in a conciliatory manner. "I really feel as if we could work this out with little to no drama."

The man glared at him through his thick glasses. "You are Maxwell Barnes?"

Max considered lying but had the distinct feeling these men, at least the smaller one in front, already knew everything there was to know about them. There was no reason to poke the bear—or, in this case, the dragon.

"Yes, that's me," Max admitted. "Do you also know why we are here?"

The man nodded, but declined to elaborate. Instead, he turned to the big gunman and rattled off a string of rapid-fire Chinese.

"Sorry, not following," Axel quipped. Max reached over and elbowed him in the ribs.

The big man nodded, obviously agreeing with whatever he had been told. Then he raised his weapon, pointed it directly at Isabel, and pulled the trigger.

Max's heart raced as he dove in front of Isabel, his body instinctively reacting to protect her. The cold, hard concrete of the parking garage met him with a jarring thud as he landed, the impact vibrating through his bones. He braced himself for the deafening roar of gunfire ...

But there was no sound.

Until there was.

And when the sound came, it was not gunshots, but the unspeakably obnoxious sound of laughter.

Max rolled over on his back and looked up at the three men. All were laughing. Uproariously ... laughing.

Quickly, he struggled up to his feet and turned to face them. His face was red with anger, and any thought of caution or diplomacy was long gone.

"What in the hell do you think you're doing!"

He looked over at Isabel and Axel, trying to gauge their reaction, and it didn't take a genius to tell they were feeling much the same. Axel's neck veins were throbbing and distended, and his massive fists clenched so hard his knuckles were white. Isabel was terrifyingly quiet and calm. Terrifying, because Max knew what this sort of deadly calm meant; it meant she was about to go apeshit crazy on someone. He struggled to regain some control, and the effort took long enough to allow the three screeching hyenas to marginally control themselves.

"We must apologize," the shorter man said, still wheezing with mirth. "This was inexcusable, but we simply could not help ourselves."

"Oh, I don't know," Max said, gritting his teeth. "I think people truly do what they want to do. So the question remains, why the hell would you want to do this?"

"It was his idea," the small man said, pointing to his largest companion. As if happy to accept the credit, the big man nodded eagerly.

A sense of sanity returned to Max, like the sun coming up after a long, dark night. His mouth dropped open, and his eyes grew wide.

"You're our contacts?"

The small man nodded. "Yes, indeed. And you should consider yourselves lucky. Not only are you getting protection and a guide into the Himalayas, but you are receiving free entertainment as well!"

Max let out a low growl. "That entertainment almost got you killed."

"Killed? I am pretty sure we are the ones with the guns."

"Yes," Axel admitted, "but you wouldn't have gotten all of us. One, maybe two, but whoever was left would've taken all of you out."

The three jokesters exchanged glances. Max could tell they were now feeling uneasy, wondering if perhaps they had gone a bit too far—the answer being obvious to him.

"You better be glad the weapon you pointed at Isabel

was indeed unloaded," he said. "Didn't anyone ever tell you to always assume a gun was loaded? So much for gun safety."

"Well, I can see our attempt at humor and a lively welcome to our country has not been appreciated," the small man said. His attitude was one of disappointment, or even annoyance their efforts had not been properly acknowledged. "I suppose we should get you to your hotel."

"That would be great," Max said. "In case you didn't know, we just completed a fourteen-hour flight out of New York and are pretty exhausted. Also, we've just come through a ridiculous situation during which we wondered if we would all be killed. Not the kind of welcome I would prefer, thank you."

"Very well," the small man said. "I'm glad to know where you all stand." He gave a sharp whistle and a grand gesture with one arm, waving them all toward the cars. "We will get you to your hotel, settled, and let you catch some hours of rest. Then we will reconvene and discuss how we are going to make it to Lhasa."

3

Everyone was understandably exhausted by the time they got to the hotel arranged for them by their thoughtless hosts. Max had intended to spend the first hour of down-time giving a heated monologue concerning the outlandish customs of this country, but as it turned out they were all too exhausted to do much of anything.

After eating some less than wonderful room service food, Max sat down at a round table at the side of the room and opened his laptop, intending to go over the files with the rest of the group. But after he fell asleep for the second time during the attempted presentation, he decided to wait until after breakfast the next day.

"Let's call it for now," he said, standing up from the table. He wobbled slightly, exhaustion threatening to shut down his system without further notice. Axel rolled off the bed where he'd been listening to Max's mumbling, and let out an enormous yawn.

"Sounds good," he said, struggling to rise to his feet. "I'm just going to wash my face real quick, and then it's off to dreamland for me." He began walking toward the bathroom, but one of his big feet caught in a lamp cord sticking out between the bed and the nightstand. The lamp, its glazed base adorned with intricate designs of traditional Chinese symbols and imagery, crashed to the floor. The lightbulb flickered but remained lit, and Axel jumped back with a yelp.

"Oh great," Max groaned. "Something else we can get charged for."

"Hey, it's not our credit card on file," Axel said defensively. "Besides, that cord was just sticking out there waiting for somebody to trip on it. You'd think they'd take those things away out of sight and out of danger. How careless."

"Boys always blaming people other than themselves," Isabel said, coming over to survey the damage. She bent down to inspect the broken shards. "You think maybe ..."

Her voice trailed off, and Max glanced over curiously. It was not like Isabel to censor her words; but then he realized she had not ceased speaking for fear of hurting their feelings, but rather was peering at the floor with a furrowed brow.

"What's up?" he asked, coming to stand over her.

"It may be a good thing you did not complete the debriefing," she said.

"What do you mean?"

Isabel looked up at him and pressed one long finger over red lips in the universal sign for silence. Then she used that same finger to point toward the floor.

At first, Max saw nothing but the broken pieces of ceramic, but then saw what Isabel was indicating.

A small, black disc lay in the middle of the destruction. A short wire poked from its side.

A transmitter, Max thought, his thoughts beginning to tumble. He reached over to the nightstand and picked up the complementary pen and pad of paper, scribbling a quick note. He held it up so the other two could see.

ACT NATURAL, it read.

"What's that you say, Isabel?" Max asked casually.

"I said it may be a good thing you did not complete the debriefing." Isabel caught on to the charade immediately. "I am too tired to listen to your ramblings. All nonsense anyway."

"Oh, give me a break," Max replied, hamming it up just a little. "I haven't slept for approximately three thousand hours."

"Well," Axel chimed in. "if you two are going to snipe at each other, I'll go wash up and head to bed. Do you need help cleaning that mess?"

"No," Isabel said, "the woman will do the work, as usual." She rolled her eyes, making Max think that this particular remark was not for the benefit of the listening device, but was some genuine commentary on her part.

As Axel went to the bathroom, Max and Isabel began to clean up the broken lamp, being careful not to disturb the small transmitter that lay among the shards. Then, they gingerly placed the device on the nightstand between the two beds and got ready to crash.

The room had two double beds and one pull-out couch,

and their hosts had only arranged for a single room. Axel got one of the beds because of his enormous size, Isabel got the other bed because Isabel, and that left Max with the couch. He was much too tired to care.

Even with the disturbing development of the bug, each of them fell asleep almost immediately, not bothering to set their alarm.

~

SOMETIME IN THE WEE HOURS, Max jerked awake at the feel of a heavy hand on his shoulder. His heart was racing faster than the lead horse at the Kentucky Derby, and his eyes started scanning around the room, scrutinizing every dark shadow.

"Shh," a voice said.

Max twisted away and hit the floor with both feet, crouched, ready to spring. His hand went to his waist for a weapon, but of course there was nothing—not only because they were in a restrictive foreign country, but because he was wearing nothing but boxers.

He turned nearly a full circle before spotting three dark figures standing in the middle of the room. One tall, one short, and one somewhere in between.

"You've got to be kidding me!" Max bellowed.

His two friends sat up in their beds and, in the same motion, Isabel came flying forward and landed like a spider monkey on the largest man's back.

He yelped in surprise and began swatting at her with both hands. She dodged every blow, clinging to his back and using her arms to put him in a chokehold. A disgusting gagging sound came from the darkness as Isabel's strategy started having its desired effect.

"Let him go!" the short figure shouted. "She'll kill him!"

Max emitted a harsh profanity. "Who cares? Axel, get the light."

Axel quickly did as requested, crossing the room with long strides and flooding it with light. As Max had suspected, there were the three men from before, only this time they were not waving weapons around.

"Isabel, stand down," Max said, his voice less of an order and more of a disappointed request, as if he would have preferred to let her finish what she had started.

Reluctantly, Isabel released her grip and slid to the floor. She backed up slowly, taking a position between Axel and Max, her burning eyes never leaving the man's still-discolored face.

Max pointed at the man with the thick glasses. "You see what happens when you sneak up on us? If this happens again, someone's going to get killed."

"I can assure you we did not intend to frighten you," the man insisted. "I do apologize profusely. However, we were forced to adopt these measures by circumstances beyond our control."

Axel grunted. "Circumstances beyond your control? Why don't I like the sound of that?"

"All is well. Nothing to worry about. We simply thought now would be a good time to embark on our trip to Lhasa."

Max barked a short, disbelieving laugh. "Now? What time is it?"

"It is two o'clock in the morning. We like to get an early start in China."

"Oh no, you don't," Max said firmly. "We are not going anywhere until you start being honest with us. What exactly is going on?"

The little man hesitated, glancing at the others, and finally turned back to Max with a resigned expression.

"Very well," he said. "We are your contacts here. There seems to have been some sort of mixup with your travel clearances."

"Go on," Max prompted, drawing out the last word.

"Yeah," Axel chimed in. "I want to hear this too."

"Some of the paperwork has not yet made it through the bureaucracy. Therefore, it is technically illegal for the three of you to travel to Lhasa."

"I want to be very clear about this," Max said. "Are you saying we *cannot* go to Lhasa, or that we *are* going the Lhasa?"

The little man cleared his throat. "We *are* going to Lhasa," he said. "It is only that we must travel more, shall we say, expeditiously."

"I like the word," Max said. "Not sure I like the concept or the insinuation. I'm also not sure I believe you about the bureaucratic red tape problem. Were our permissions delayed ... or denied?"

"Well, both, actually," the man said.

"How can it be both?" Axel asked, moving forward and taking two full steps.

The little man held up his hand. "I'll tell you the truth," he said. "The clearances had not yet been fully approved by the time the three of you made final plans to visit Lhasa. However, it was expected that by the time you arrived, we would have the necessary paperwork."

"I see," Max said. "Guessing that didn't actually happen."

"Unfortunately, no. And now we are in the unenviable position of having to either wait and hope everything comes through in our favor, or simply continue and let the chips fall where they may."

"Any clue how long that will take?"

The man shook his head. "No idea. And, of course, there is no guarantee any of this will work out in your favor."

Axel frowned. "When you say 'in our favor,' are you saying it's simply a matter of yes or a no? Or is there something more important at stake?"

"Yeah, I was wondering that same thing," Max said. "There's something in your tone I don't like, little guy."

"The name is Ruo," the man said.

Axel brightened. "Hey, they have names! Let's keep the party going." He pointed at the big man.

"Wei," the man said.

Axel pointed at the third and final man.

"Han."

Axel gave a sarcastic slow clap. "Now we're all good pals and you can tell us the truth, as my buddy Max has already requested."

Ruo sighed again. "Things may have been done in haste."

"Such as?"

"Such as your bookings and arrangements for Lhasa.

You see, a foreigner is not allowed to make full arrangements for Tibet without first receiving official permissions. It is considered presumption and not viewed favorably."

"Especially for Americans?"

Ruo simply shrugged.

Now it was Max's turn to sigh. "So, basically, what you're telling us is we are screwed either way. Whether we get approved or denied, we've already made a grave error by presuming upon Tibetan hospitality."

"It is not so much the Tibetans, as it is the Chinese government," Ruo said. "But in any case, yes, I am afraid you are correct, at least in the main."

"And the consequences?"

"The government can be capricious," Ruo said ominously. "I would not want to place my fate in their hands."

"I'm going to make another assumption," Max said. "The fact you came here in the dead of night makes me think you have some reason to believe things are about to get dangerous. Am I right? Honest answers only, please."

There were no honest answers forthcoming. In fact, there were no answers at all. The room was dead silent for two full minutes. But that was answer enough for Max.

"Okay, guys," he said. "We are getting the hell out of here."

4

Situated at an altitude of 11,450 feet above sea level, making it one of the highest cities in the world, Lhasa is the capital and largest city of the Tibet Autonomous Region. Known for its unique blend of Tibetan and Chinese cultures, it is considered one of the most important religious and cultural centers in Tibet.

Lhasa is surrounded by towering mountains, including the majestic Mount Everest, and the Brahmaputra River flows through the valley below. The city's streets are lined with colorful traditional Tibetan buildings, many of which are adorned with intricate carvings and murals. The most famous of these is the Potala Palace, former residence of the Dalai Lama.

It was into this picturesque population center that Max, Axel, and Isabel landed in the mid-morning. After being hustled from their hotel in the dead of night, their increasingly suspicious hosts had driven them to a remote landing strip, where a small plane was waiting, engines already going.

The flight took several hours, but as they approached their destination, all three adventurers had to admit the scene before them was absolutely breathtaking. As the first rays of sunlight peeked over the horizon behind them, the sky was painted in a vibrant array of colors, from soft pink and orange hues to deep reds and purples. The snow-capped peaks of the mountains ahead were illuminated by the warm light, casting a golden glow over the landscape.

As the sun rose higher, the colors changed. The snow-capped peaks turned into a dazzling white, the glaciers and ice fields started to sparkle, and the shadows slowly retreated. The rugged terrain of the mountains was revealed in all its glory, with jagged peaks and deep valleys as the world awakened from its slumber, and the mountains stood tall, majestic, and unyielding.

The plane landed at another small airstrip on the outskirts of the city. There, transportation was waiting in the form of one of the black cars they had seen in the parking garage. Talk had been limited throughout the entire trip, and nothing of real substance, and this trend continued during the car ride into the city.

"Where to now?" Max asked. "Hotel? Gulag? Firing squad?"

Ruo laughed. "I am so glad we got guests with a sense of humor," he said. "A good-natured lightheartedness will make the task before us that much more bearable."

"Well, that's kind of why I'm asking. What exactly is the task before us? I mean, I know why we *originally* came here, but I'm getting a feeling perhaps our objectives have been altered without our permission."

"The first order of business is to feed you some traditional Tibetan fare," Ruo said. "We will drop you at a recommended eatery and leave you for a while. I'm sure you all have much to discuss."

Max considered mentioning the listening device they had found in the hotel room, but decided against it. For all he knew, these men were the ones who put it there, and he would prefer whoever placed the bug remain in the dark regarding the device's discovery.

Instead, he muttered, "How thoughtful."

He had to admit he was absolutely ravenous, and he was certain the other two were as well—especially Axel, who practically ate his body weight on a daily basis.

As the car wound and joggled its way down a stretch of cobblestone road, Max looked out at the surroundings. The street was lined with shops, stalls, and vendors selling a wide range of goods, everything from traditional Tibetan clothing, jewelry, and crafts, to religious items such as prayer flags and incense. The buildings along the road were mostly constructed of stone and mud brick, reaching up several stories. Despite the hustle and bustle of the street, however, the atmosphere was peaceful and serene, with locals going about their daily lives with a sense of calm and contentment—much different from the intensity of Shanghai, and more to Max's taste. He had traveled much of the world, but was not what many might call "worldly," and while he'd been involved in many dangerous and high-stakes situations, he also loved solitude and peace.

Ruo pulled to the side of the road and tapped sharply on the steering wheel.

"Out you go!" he chirped.

The three explorers did not have to be told twice, and they all scrambled out of the vehicle on the curb-side. Axel slammed the car door shut and the vehicle roared away. Max turned to look at the restaurant in front of them. The exterior was simple and unassuming, with a small sign hanging above the door bearing the name of the establishment: The Snow Lotus.

Upon entering, they were greeted by a local woman who spoke surprisingly good English. After being seated, they asked to be served some of the local favorites, to which the woman smiled, nodded, and disappeared into the back of the restaurant.

"I'm guessing she gets that request a lot," Axel said. "A lot of international mountain climbers come through here to try their luck with the Himalayas. And I'm guessing not all of them are up to speed on Tibetan cuisine."

"I'm not either," Max said. "But perhaps I should've studied up."

"I do not care what they bring us," Isabel said.

Max noticed her face was back to shining with excitement, and she was smiling broadly. He loved this look on her, like that of an eager schoolgirl, hopeful to see the world and experience new things. It was not something he had seen from her very often; she was usually much more focused, serious, and sometimes frighteningly intense. But this was something different, and Max enjoyed every minute of it.

Speaking of love, Paranoia piped up. *Seems to me you're headed pretty fast in that exact direction.*

On one level, Max thought it strange Paranoia would be the one to bring up such a topic, but he had to admit actually falling in love with somebody *was* something he feared deep down. And, to be honest, it was not something with which he had vast experience. After his mother died when he was young, Max was left in the care of his father who, although kind, had not been overly affectionate. Professor Anderson Barnes was not exactly a cold man, but he kept his emotions hidden deep beneath a thick exterior of academic decorum. Somehow, even though Axel had been raised alongside Max when taken in by Professor Barnes, the bigger man had managed to retain much of his emotional intelligence. Perhaps it was because Axel was just a couple of years older than Max, or maybe it had something to do with his hot Latin blood. Whatever it was, Max wondered if he might need to have a conversation with his best friend before too long. A conversation about romance ... love? ... and what to do about it.

The food arrived with pleasantly speedy service, and the three tucked in without preamble. The delightful and authentic combination of momos, thukpa, and tsampa was comforting and warmed them from inside out.

Finally, they all sat back, their faces flushed with the joy of a comfortably full stomach.

"Oh good lord," Axel rumbled. "I don't know if that was the best thing I've ever eaten, but it is definitely in the top ten."

"Top three for me," Max said, wishing they could

somehow get a to-go box. But he had no idea where they were headed next and assumed it would not be somewhere conducive to such comfort as provided by this restaurant.

Isabel said nothing, but the satisfied and serene expression on her face let Max know she shared their assessment of the meal.

"Ready to go?"

They all jumped, and then Max noticed Ruo standing just off to the side, his hands clasped behind his back, and that good-natured smile—which Max was quickly coming to find obnoxious—plastered across his face. The man's eyes goggled behind his thick glasses, and one eyebrow went up in query. Behind him stood Wei and Han, both looking impassive and statuesque.

"Little man," Axel said, his voice deadly serious, "if you don't stop sneaking up on us, I am going to throw you into the nearest river."

"No need for violence," Ruo said. "I am merely here to tell you we have your quarters for the night, and we will leave tomorrow for basecamp."

"Basecamp?" Max crossed his arms over his chest. "Does this mean we are actually now getting on with the real mission?"

"Indeed!"

"How about my friends and I take a moment to look for some souvenirs? This is a great town."

Ruo scrunched up his face. "I am afraid that will not be allowed. Perhaps later today."

"Okay," Axel said. "Two things wrong with that statement. First of all, nobody tells me what I am *not* allowed to do. Second thing, why are we always having to leave places in such a hurry? Can't we take a minute and relax?"

"You may relax in your quarters and when we reach basecamp," Ruo said. "Then there will be no reason for haste."

Max sighed. "So why the haste now?"

At that moment, he glanced out the front windows of the restaurant and noticed two very official-looking men ambling down the other side of the street. They affected an extreme attitude of nonchalance, which let Max know they were actually up to something. As he watched, they stopped at every storefront and peered in through the glass, shading their eyes from the glare of the sun, as if surveying all the faces inside. Max nodded his head in their direction and then looked at Ruo suspiciously.

"Our departure doesn't happen to have anything to do with those two, does it?"

Ruo's expression did not change at all, and he did not reply. Instead, he walked past the group and headed toward the rear of the restaurant. As Han and Wei followed behind him, the biggest Chinese man mumbled,

"Follow us."

~

THEIR CHINESE GUIDES led the way through the twisting, narrow back alleys of Lhasa. Max and the others continually looked over their shoulders, around corners before they traversed crossroads, and generally kept as low a profile as possible. They must have made a suspicious sight, for several people glanced at them curiously as they scuttled past. At one point, a man in some sort of religious garb spoke to Ruo, who chattered something in reply and waved him away.

"What did he say?" Max asked, worried perhaps they had been discovered.

"He asked if we needed sanctuary," Ruo said, shaking his head in disgust.

"Uh, I'm not so sure we don't," Axel grunted. "Is it too late to call him back?"

Ruo huffed, partly from annoyance and partly from the fact they had been hustling for some time now. "We are almost there," he said.

Just past the next street, they came to a three-story, mud-brick building supported by immense timbers. Max had no way to discern the ages of local buildings, but this place looked old. Ruo walked up to a door in the side of the building and opened it without knocking. He waved the others through before entering himself and closing the door.

They found themselves in a big, open room that reminded Max of a medieval dining hall. It certainly appeared to be communal in nature. There were two rows of beds around the outer edges, and in the center was a large table lined with chairs. The ceiling was adorned with wooden carvings, depicting scenes of the local culture and mythology, while the air inside the room carried the scent of burning juniper and other herbs, adding to the cozy and welcoming atmosphere.

"This is not what I had in mind for accommodations,"

Max said. He looked over at Isabel, expecting to see the mother of all storms ready to make landfall. To his surprise, the excited expression she had been sporting lately remained. "Don't tell me you're down with this."

The woman turned to him, still smiling. "It is essential Tibetan experience," she said. "Sharing, community—" she drew in a deep breath of the fragrant air "—we will just soak it all in."

Max stared at her in disbelief. "Okay, who are you and what have you done with Isabel?"

Isabel's childlike excitement during the entire trip had before given him a great deal of enjoyment, but this was taking it a little too far and was beginning to make him suspicious.

She's up to something, Paranoia piped up.

"Isn't she always?" Max said.

"Excited?" Axel answered. "Not really. I'm not sure I've *ever* seen Isabel excited. At least, not over something that didn't involve using her knife to dispatch a bad guy."

Max felt a little surge of reassurance that his friend was noticing the same thing as he was.

"Unfortunately, this is all we could arrange on such short notice," Ruo said. "We did, however, manage to get you semi-private quarters on the second floor."

"Hear that, Isabel?" Max asked. "No more community."

She shrugged. "I am thinking you are trying to harden the softness."

"Two things," Max said. "First of all, I think you mean 'harshen the mellow,' and second of all, that's what she said."

Isabel reached over and punched Max hard on the arm. He grinned. It definitely hurt, but that was something the old Isabel would have done, and the familiarity was comforting.

"This way," Ruo said, waving them onward. He led the way up a nearby flight of stairs to the second floor and to a doorway just off to the right of the landing.

"This is the room for the men," he said, "and there is an adjoining door for the convenience of the lady."

He opened the door and then stepped back so Max and the others could enter.

"Oh, I like this," Axel said, surveying the room with pleasant surprise.

The room was unexpectedly spacious and featured two queen-size beds with comforters featuring traditional designs. The floor was bare wood, but it was clear that was a feature, not a bug, with various animal skins scattered around to create a cozy atmosphere. The windows in the room were small, but let in sufficient light, and were adorned with wooden shutters, which could be closed for privacy. There was a fireplace on one wall but had a fixed grate in front of it, which made Max think perhaps it was not for public use. On the wall hung regional curiosities: snowshoes, mountain climbing gear, and some black-and-white photographs of unidentified mountaineers. In the center of the room was a hefty wooden table, surrounded by four chairs, which seemed to be the focal point of the room. The table was made of dark, polished wood and had carvings on its legs and edges.

Ruo walked to a door set into the wall opposite the fireplace and opened it as well. "And for the lady," he said.

The second room was a smaller version of the first, with much of the same decor but with a more feminine flare. The room featured an extra piece of furniture in the form of a handcrafted wooden dresser, and was short one queen bed.

"Fair enough," Max said with grudging appreciation. "Maybe you didn't do so bad after all, Ruo."

Ruo just smiled.

"It was about time you came through," Axel huffed. "We are guests, after all."

"I hope you enjoy your stay," Ruo said, giving a slight nod. "Tomorrow, we will head for the basecamp."

Max pumped his fist and grinned broadly. "And then the real fun can begin!"

5

"ALL RIGHT," MAX SAID, OPENING HIS LAPTOP AND SETTING IT on the remarkably ornate table. He pulled out one chair and sat down, then began working on the computer, bringing up all the important documents he had scanned during the flight to Shanghai. Axel and Isabel came over and joined him, pulling out chairs for themselves.

"Yeah, I guess it is time we started making the actual plans," Axel said. "And by the way, I think it's high time you acknowledged what good friends Isabel and I are. All we had to hear was 'ancient scroll' and we were totally on board."

Max nodded. "I will admit you both are great friends. But I don't think that's the reason you agreed to come along on this expedition. You two just can't resist adventure. Which I totally get, by the way."

Isabel scooted her chair closer, the leg screeching on the

hardwood floor. "You will stop speaking nonsense now and tell us the details. I have greatly enjoyed the trip, but I have to admit, some strange things have been happening."

"Well, I hate to disappoint you," Max said. "But I don't have any answers regarding the bizarre happenings since we landed. However, I can tell you some details about why we're here and what I hope to accomplish while we're here."

"Good," Axel said. "Then let's get to it."

Max turned his laptop so the other two would have an easier time viewing the documents. On the desktop were several open files: a PDF, three images, and a paused media player app. Max pointed to the screen, indicating the PDF file.

"This is reportedly a translated portion of the scroll. The accuracy is in question, given the language is not fully known and appears to be some sort of combination of various ancient dialects."

Isabel leaned closer. "It does not seem to make much sense," she said, squinting as if narrowed eyes would make the words more decipherable. The translated text was certainly in English, but the sentence structure and syntax were almost nonsensical.

"Unfortunately, the scholars I consulted did not know enough about the language itself to perform a contextual translation. Instead, this is sort of a word-for-word translation, with a good deal of guesswork thrown in. As a result, it doesn't make a lot of sense unless you take some pretty great liberties to read between the lines."

Axel hummed. "I'm definitely seeing many words like 'beginning,' 'origin,' and 'before.'"

"Yes, exactly," Max said. "As I told you back in the States, this is described as the Origin Scroll, because scholars believe it describes the beginning of, well, everything."

"And what are those?" Isabel asked, pointing to the images on the screen.

"Those are photographs of the actual scroll. As you can see, it's in pretty rough shape and is incomplete. Plus, some of the text itself has either been faded or eaten away by insects."

"Well, that certainly wouldn't help in constructing the aforementioned context," Axel said.

"Exactly."

"So, if they already have the scroll," Axel wondered aloud. "Why are we here? From the little you told us in the States, I gathered the scroll is actually what we were after."

"It is," Max said cryptically. "You see, there is reported to be another scroll. This one is intact, written in a more common language, and possibly containing further details not even contained in this scroll before it was partially destroyed."

Axel's eyes lit up. "Oh, now I'm getting it. This could be good."

Max nodded. "I'm hoping so. The trick is going to be not pissing off the locals. I was hoping to keep a pretty low profile during the entire trip, but the hijinks from our Chinese guides have definitely complicated that. Not to mention the fact we seem to have picked up a tail."

"Oh, you mean those two bozos out in the street when we were at the restaurant?"

"You noticed them too, huh?"

Axel snorted. "Only a rank amateur wouldn't have noticed them. They were so obvious they might as well have been wearing sandwich boards that said, 'Hello, I'm here to track your every move.'"

Max chuckled. "As Isabel said, lots of strange things have been happening. I honestly don't know what to make of it. But I say we continue on and just keep a close eye on everything and everyone. I don't think we are particularly welcome here by the powers that be."

"And what is that?" Isabel asked, as usual being the one to redirect the situation back to business. She pointed to the media player on the screen.

"Ah," Max said. "That is a recording reported to be the voice of the last person who tried to find the second Origin Scroll."

"That entire sentence made me really uncomfortable," Axel said.

"And it should," Max agreed. "You think you're uncomfortable now, wait until you hear it." Using the laptop's trackpad, he moved the cursor and hovered over the play button. "Are you ready for this?" He looked at the other two, his face absolutely serious.

"From the way you're acting, I'm guessing not," Axel said. "But let's do it anyway."

Max nodded and pressed play.

There were a few seconds of silence, populated only by the hiss and scratch of heavy static.

I am alone, and the storm has been raging for days. My Sherpa guide disappeared just before the storm, and I have not seen him since. Two days ago, I thought I might be able to make it down from the mountain during a brief respite from the storm. But some ... thing, forced me back into this cave. A lion, maybe ... or a bear, but I don't think so. Something much bigger, something fiercer, something ... smarter.

I was forced to retreat back to the cave, where I remained still and quiet, using ash from the fire to disguise my scent. Whatever it was, it finally went away, but by then the storm had returned with all its fury, and I could not leave the shelter. That was the last time I attempted to descend.

New snow has stopped falling, but the wind still blows so fiercely that it is impossible to see more than a foot or two ahead of you. Without my guide, I would undoubtedly fall into a crevasse or tumble down an incline. If I were to injure myself on the descent, that would be the end of it. I am still hopeful that the storm will settle in time, but I fear that when it does ... the creature will return.

The man paused, then continued.

But perhaps the wind is settling now. I will look from the mouth of the cave.

There was a thumping sound as the speaker set down the microphone or other recording device. More silence.

And then Max tapped the pause button.

"Is that it?" Axel asked.

Max avoided his friend's questioning gaze. "Not quite."

"Then let's hear the rest of it!" the big man demanded. "No more games—I'm sick of that crap!"

Max shook his head. "No games. I just ... I'm not sure I can listen to this part again."

Axel immediately sobered. "That bad?"

"That bad."

A pause.

Then Isabel said softly, "Max, we must hear it."

Max sighed, nodded, and then tapped the button to resume play.

The static started up at once, but for several more seconds, there was nothing else to be heard. And then, echoing in the distance, they all heard a long, wailing cry that seemed to travel through every valley, bouncing off every peak. It started low, a guttural growl that came from deep within the earth. But as it grew louder, the pitch rose, and with it, the sense of malevolence. It was a wail, but also a threat—a promise of violence and destruction, carrying a heavy undertone of aggressive malice. As it reached a crescendo, Max felt—as he did every time he heard it—a crackling chill run up his spine, and a cold, creeping fear seemed to grip him with icy claws.

And then a scream.

A human scream.

And the static stopped.

"Boy, did I ever need this," Axel said, holding up his cup of chang as they sat in a local bar not far from their rooms. "Also, this might be my new favorite beer."

"It's not bad," Max agreed, examining his own portion. The traditional Tibetan beer had a cloudy appearance and a tangy, slightly sour taste. "I hear it's good for altitude sickness, so let's drink up. We'll be climbing soon enough."

Axel peered over the brim of his cup while he drank. "We're still doing that, huh?"

"The recording?"

"What else? And now I know why you kept that stuff from us until we arrived. You were probably worried if we heard it beforehand, we might have refused to come along. And, you know what? You might have been right."

Max nodded. "It's terrifying, that's for sure."

"Where did the recording come from?" Isabel asked, taking a sip from her cup of chang.

"It's from the late 1930s," Max replied. "Apparently, some explorer had set up a camp high in the Himalayas, complete with a radio transmitter. He was communicating with the main camp in the valley. Against the advice of his colleagues, he made a trip to the upper outpost by himself. A bad storm blew in and trapped him there. It was too dangerous for anyone to try to find him. Anyway, he got trapped there, but was able to send reports. Somehow, his receiver got damaged, so he could transmit messages but couldn't receive anything. As it started to become more obvious things were going badly, the basecamp crew started recording his transmissions. The one I played for you was the final they received."

"That is absolutely chilling," Axel said. He looked around for anyone who appeared willing to refill his chang. "So, these explorers were looking for the Origin Scroll?"

"So it would seem. But after this tragedy, their funding was pulled and they were forced to abandon the expedition.

Plus, the world was teetering on the brink of war and everybody was feeling a bit on edge."

Axel looked down at his cup, and as if by magic, it was refilled. "So, are we actually going to do this or not?"

"Well, we certainly don't have to," Max said. "I don't want to drag the two of you into something you don't want to do."

Isabel snorted. "Now you say this, after you bring us here under false pretenses."

"False pretenses!" Max exclaimed. "I didn't lie. I simply carefully curated the information and presented it to you."

Axel burst out laughing. "I guess it all depends on what the definition of 'is' is, doesn't it? But let's be real about this. Both Isabel and I would've been on board no matter what. As terrifying, bizarre, and quite clearly dangerous as this mission is turning out to be, you wouldn't have been able to beat us off with a stick. Frankly, the only thing I'm bothered by is that you didn't trust us enough to tell everything upfront."

Max could see his point. "I hear you. And I should probably also tell you there is some speculation this recording is fake."

"If that's fake, it's a damn good one," Axel said.

"I agree," Max said. "But there is an academic faction that believes it to be a fraud."

"Faction?" Isabel asked. "Are we now talking about Professor Barnes?"

"How did you know?" Max asked sardonically.

Isabel didn't answer, but she didn't need to.

Axel tossed back the rest of his refilled chang. "So, who's funding this particular mission, if not the Prof's university?"

This time it was Max's turn not to answer a question, and Axel looked at him, raising an eyebrow.

"Max?" he said, his voice taking on a deadly serious tone. "Who's funding this mission?"

6

"Crabtree," Axel roared. "Okay, now I'm pissed. I cannot believe you didn't tell us!"

They had left the bar behind, and Axel's booming voice echoed through the streets of Lhasa.

"Quiet!" Max hissed, reaching over to punch Axel's musclebound arm. "We're trying to maintain a low profile, remember?"

"Maxwell," Isabel said, using his full name as she often did when absolutely furious with him. "I would stab you with my grandmother's knife, if I had it. But still, you had better sleep lightly from now on!"

"Look, guys," Max pleaded. "At first, the university was going to fund this, and that's when I told you all about it and asked you to go along. Then the funding fell through for some reason, and I was left hanging."

"Forget the university," Axel said. He was trying to whisper, but Axel's version of a whisper was equivalent to some people's normal volume. "I'm more interested in the fact that he's not, you know, *dead!*"

"No one could have been more surprised than I was," Max said.

"So you didn't make contact with him?"

"No. He made contact with me."

"How do we know we can believe that? At the rate you're eroding the trust of this group, we may not be able to believe anything anyone says ever again!"

"Okay, I understand you're upset," Max allowed. "But let's not get overwrought, shall we?"

"Maxwell, do you not remember everything Crabtree did to us?" Isabel said. "He kidnapped my abuela! And think of Axel!"

This statement took all the wind out of Max's sails. Not that he hadn't understood where they were coming from before, but this perspective hit him between the eyes. He remembered only too well their adventures in Guatemala and the deep trauma his best friend had suffered at the hands of his lover, who had been used as a pawn by Myron Crabtree. A deep shame washed through him, and he stopped dead in his tracks. He turned toward Axel, but couldn't meet his eyes.

"Ax ... buddy ..."

Axel reached out with one massive paw and placed it on Max's shoulder. "I know you didn't mean it that way," he said. "But ... damn, dude."

Max felt a lump in his throat, taken aback as he so often was by Axel's gentle nature. "I know. I—"

"And my abuela?" Isabel interrupted.

"I'm sorry about that too," Max said honestly. "But guys—this mission. This could be crazy huge!"

Both his friends stood, staring at him silently.

"Guys? Say something?" Max pleaded.

Axel, who still had a grip on Max's shoulder, began squeezing until Max began squirming from the pain. "Listen, Maxy—we're here now. And we know you'd never intentionally hurt us. But seriously—you cannot keep secrets like this from us anymore. Got it?"

Max nodded. "Fair enough. More than fair, actually. And I am sorry. But also, don't call me Maxy."

And then the group was laughing.

"Just speaking for myself," Axel said, growing just a bit more serious again. "I'm mostly upset you didn't loop us in right away. It does sometimes feel as if you don't see us as full partners in this entire thing. Being fully honest, I think you need to do some work in that area."

Max felt a little twinge of defensiveness, but he forced it down. His friend was absolutely correct. "Guys, I'm sorry. If you want to head back now, I would completely understand. No hard feelings, nothing will change, and I'll make sure you're compensated for any expenses you may have incurred."

Isabel and Axel looked at each other, and then slowly as one, they began to grin once more.

"I think he's on to us," Axel said.

Isabel nodded. "I think so as well."

"What are you two talking about?" Max demanded, frowning. "I'm being serious."

"You sure you're not calling our bluff?" Axel said.

"Bluff?"

"Come on, Maxy," Axel said. "It's not like you to offer a heartfelt apology about anything. You know very well we would've come along no matter what. And so you didn't even feel it that necessary to bring it up. Right?"

Max looked at the ground and stubbed his toe on a cobblestone. "Not exactly," he said. "But that reasoning did make me feel a lot less guilty about it." Then he started grinning. "Oh, and for the last time. Don't call me—"

"Maxy," all three said in unison.

And so the trio stood in the middle of a cobblestone street in Lhasa, Tibet, laughing so hard they drew stares from nearly everyone who passed them by.

"Okay," Max said finally, bending over with his hands on his knees, trying to take a full breath. "Let's get back to the room. I want to check on a couple of things and then we need to go shopping to replace all the gear we lost when the taxi drove off. Including our damn sat phone, by the way."

"And I would like to buy a knife," Isabel said ominously.

The hostel was just one street away, and they entered by the same door shown to them by Ruo earlier. Up the stairs to the second floor they went, Max's spirits lighter than they had been since before they arrived in Shanghai. He was practically bursting with pride and affection for his companions, and he made a pledge to never take them for granted again.

As they reached the door to the room, Max's hand gripped the knob, and at that same moment he heard, rather than felt, the toe of his boot step into something sticky and wet. He glanced down at the floor and froze.

"What's up?" Axel asked.

Wordlessly, Max pointed toward the floor, and then heard Axel's low and profane exhalation.

"Is that what I think it is?" Isabel asked.

Max nodded. "If you think it's blood."

"Maybe we shouldn't go in," Axel suggested. "Whoever did this might still be waiting inside."

Max shook his head. "No, I don't think so. But if you want to stand aside while I open the door, that's probably a good idea."

Isabel and Axel took the suggestion, each pressing their backs to one side of the door, their palms pressed flat against the wall, ready to whirl inside at a moment's notice.

Max took a deep breath, turned the knob, and pushed the door open.

The sight that met his eyes was not something he ever wished to see again. It was, if possible, even worse than the time in Guatemala when he'd seen a man with the skin of his back flayed completely off.

"It's Wei," he said, his voice dull.

"Anyone else around?" Axel asked.

"Not that I can tell. It looks clear, other than this gruesome mess on the floor."

He moved deeper into the room, skirting around the shockingly large pool of blood beneath the headless body of Wei. The other two followed behind. Axel closed the door after them and stared at the body.

"How can you tell it's Wei?" Axel asked. "He's not the only large man in this town, surely."

Without answering, Max pointed to the table. There,

directly in the center, was Wei's missing head. The eyes were open, staring blankly, and something—Max couldn't quite tell what—protruded from the head's gaping mouth.

Axel emitted a sound of deep disgust. Not quite a gag, but something that communicated not only a physical level of revulsion but also a visceral rejection of such brutality.

"Well, that's something I never need to see again," he said, employing his standard procedure of making light of horrendous situations.

Max move toward the table—and the head—and took a closer look at whatever protruded from the mouth.

"It's a rolled-up piece of paper." Reaching out, he gingerly tugged the paper free. It had been rolled in the manner of a scroll and tied in the middle with a short length of ribbon. "Oh, a scroll. How clever."

He untied one end of the ribbon, and it came loose easily. He unrolled it, trying not to think about where it had recently been deposited. He stared at the paper for an indeterminate length of time, until finally Axel prompted,

"Well? What does it say?"

Max handed over the paper, and Axel looked at it, frowning.

"Well?" Isabel asked.

Axel shrugged, handing her the paper. "It's just one word," he said. "But it's pretty clear, nonetheless."

"LEAVE," Isabel read. "It says only: LEAVE."

"And that is exactly what you should do," a voice spoke from the gloom, galvanizing all three explorers into action.

As one unit, they turned toward the voice, each dropping into a fighting stance, ready to do battle with whatever monster was about to attack. Then, just as suddenly, they came up short. Before them stood Ruo. His glasses were missing, his thinning hair was mussed, and he held up his shaking hands as if pleading for mercy.

"What the hell happened here?" Max demanded. "If you don't tell us right now, you're going to die. We're tired of messing around with this shit. We're done playing."

"Please," Ruo begged, falling to his knees. "I did not do this."

"Then who did?"

"It was Han. He has betrayed us and led attackers here to the hostel. I heard them coming and managed to hide, but unfortunately, Wei was not as lucky."

"I'm still not getting it," Max said. "Why were the three of you split up in the first place?"

"Han had said he was going out to buy some gear to replace what was taken by the taxi driver. But when he came back, it was not with supplies but rather with ... them."

"Them?" Isabel said. "And who is them?"

Ruo still kneeled there, trembling from head to toe, his face a ghastly white. "May I rise?"

"Oh, for Pete's sake," Max grunted. "Nobody asked you to fall on your knees in the first place, you weirdo. Just tell us what's going on."

Ruo struggled to his feet, and it was then Max saw a glint of metal on the floor a few feet away.

A pistol.

"Isabel," he said calmly, pointing to the weapon, "would you mind grabbing that?"

Isabel followed the point and saw it immediately. Walking over, she scooped it up, casting Ruo a dirty look.

"It was not mine!" the man insisted. "Wei must have dropped it."

No one bothered to reply.

Ruo stood there for a moment, and then turned to point toward the laptop that still sat on the table not far from Wei's head. Max made a mental note to buy a new computer as soon as possible—one that had not shared space with a decapitated head.

"I happened to see a bit of your research," Ruo said. "Including the audio file. So I assume you have some knowledge of the Migoi."

"Uh, nope," Max said. "Not unless you're talking about whatever made that horrible noise at the end."

Ruo nodded. "That is it exactly."

"I've never heard of a Migoi," Axel said. "What is that, some sort of evil spirit?"

Ruo was still trembling. "I wish I could tell you everything, but we should all leave this place."

"I agree," Max said. "Let's grab some gear real quick and get to the basecamp. I'm starting to feel like that's the only place we'll be safe."

"Basecamp!" Ruo said. "Surely you jest!"

"Surely I don't," Max said, shrugging. "Any reason why we shouldn't?"

Ruo looked around the room, meaningfully scanning the body, the head, the sea of blood. Then he looked back at Max, his face a study in confusion.

Despite his surroundings, Max smiled—but it was a grim sort of smile.

“There’s something you should know about us, Ruo. We don’t scare easy. In fact, we don’t scare at all. In fact again, the more attempts to scare us off, the more determined we get. So, yeah, this is an awful thing that has happened—” and here he motioned to the unfortunate Wei “—but this just tells me we’re on to something worth being on to. Now, come on. You can tell us about the Migoi on the way out to camp.”

7

THE RATTLING SUV TRUNDLED ACROSS THE ROUGH TERRAIN as Max and the crew headed toward basecamp. Ruo, the only one of the current group who knew the location of the camp, was at the wheel, and he stared out the front windshield with the intensity of a man who worried his time on earth was limited.

Max desperately wanted to discuss the situation with Isabel, but some of what he had to say involved Ruo, and it wouldn't do to have the man eavesdrop on that particular conversation. He had deep doubts about Ruo's story concerning what happened at the hostel. It was certainly possible, but at this point, Max didn't know whom to trust. Was Ruo simply a coward, or had he actually been involved in the betrayal that killed Wei? And why had Wei been killed?

There were other questions on Max's mind he did not wish to explore. He was beginning to have sneaking suspicions regarding the timing of the funding cancellation by the university. Had it all simply been a bureaucratic mess-up or was there something more sinister at work—something that just happened to coincide with their lack of travel clearance once they arrived in Shanghai?

So many questions ...

Some things they *could* talk about in Ruo's presence, however, including the mysterious Migoi. As it turned out, the Migoi was another name for a yeti, as Max found out with a quick internet search. Yet, he felt there was more to it than that, so he leaned forward in his seat.

"Ruo, back in Lhasa, you mentioned something about Han coming back with 'them.' What did you mean by 'them?'"

Ruo was silent for a moment, clutching the steering wheel with white-knuckled hands and staring out the windshield, his eyes intent on the landscape. At last, he drew in a deep breath and relaxed his grip on the wheel just the barest amount—enough so at least a little blood ran back into his hands.

"I was talking about the Migoi," he said.

Max frowned. "The Migoi? I thought the Migoi was the yeti. Are you telling me there's a number of them running around Lhasa?"

"No, not that. The Migoi is the name of the creature, yes. But it is also the name of the creature's followers. They also call themselves the Migoi."

"So it can be both singular *and* plural. Like moose."

"Moose?" Isabel looked at him. "Is not the plural of moose 'meese'?"

Max grinned. "No, but it should be. But getting back to the meese, er, Migoi, that's just exactly what we needed on this little expedition."

"Let me guess," Axel chimed in. "These Migoi have something to do with the scroll, don't they?"

Ruo glanced in the rearview mirror, giving Isabel a quick look of appreciation.

"Indeed," he admitted. "The Migoi have, for centuries, considered themselves the protectors of not only the Himalayas but also the creature and the scroll. It is their belief the Migoi itself was the beginning of all things, and that life began here in the mountains."

"And is this what the Origin Scroll claims?" Max asked.

"Nobody knows for sure," Ruo said. "Not in the version we have now. But it has been long rumored that the second Origin Scroll—the one containing the more complete account of the beginning of all things—does indeed make such a claim."

"You know," Max said. "I always say every adventure can be improved when you add a dash of fanaticism. Looks like we have that in spades."

"The Migoi is nothing to mess with," Ruo said seriously.

"The creature or its followers?"

"Either. And on the subject of the expedition, I feel it prudent to inform you that those at the basecamp are likely unaware of the change in circumstances."

"Which change?" Axel asked. "There have been quite a few."

"I speak of the change in authorization," Ruo said diplomatically. "This particular camp is a research facility sponsored by the university at which Professor Anderson Barnes works. As the present Mr. Barnes is aware, that is where the funding was originally going to come from. However, when the funding was pulled, the staff currently at the basecamp were informed they would no longer be receiving visitors."

"I see," Max said, frowning. "So, you're saying they might be a little surprised to see us."

"Indeed," Ruo said again.

Max sat back in his seat. In direct contradiction of his feelings, he displayed a cocky grin and said,

"Well, I suppose we should all get our stories straight."

THE SUV CAME TO A SHAKING, squeaking halt just inside the entry to basecamp. Max followed the others as they exited the vehicle and took a few moments to stretch their tight muscles. He walked around to the front of the SUV and surveyed their surroundings.

The research camp was in the heart of the Himalayas, at the base of a mountain range. It was fairly small, but appeared functional and reasonably well-equipped. It was not a bustling place, but Max hadn't expected it to be, especially since they weren't expecting visitors.

The camp was set up in a clearing, surrounded by towering peaks. Had it been established too much farther on, it would have been accessible only by foot or helicopter. As it was, there had been a couple of tense moments near the end of the drive during which Max had been certain they were going to get stuck or roll off the side of a ravine.

The camp consisted of a few large tents and two more permanent structures. These were constructed roughly of wood planking and resembled a few upgraded hunting shacks Max had witnessed during various deer seasons back in the States.

Off to the side, Max noticed a row of three portable toilets and a small shower tent. He could hear the rumble of a generator somewhere at the back of the camp, and atop the largest structure was a solar panel.

The camp appeared to be located in a strategic position, providing a good view of the surrounding area to allow the group to keep an eye out for any potential dangers. Max had not been joking when he'd said earlier that basecamp might be the only safe place for them. It would take a dedicated stalker indeed to travel all the way out here, even if they knew its location, and this was one place they may be able defend, if it came to that.

As Max completed his assessment, the front door of the smaller wooden structure banged open and an immense man lumbered out. He held a rifle in his hands and, as they watched, he pointed it up into the air and pulled the trigger.

"Halt!" he roared. "One more step and I'll blow your damn heads off!"

Max glanced over at Ruo, expected him to take the lead, but the little guy seemed in no hurry to head off the man. Gathering himself, Max stepped forward, plastering a disarming smile on his face.

"Hello, sir!" Max said, keeping his voice light and friendly. "We're the exploration crew from the university. I'm sure you're expecting us." It was a bit of a reckless gamble, but under the circumstances, Max didn't see what choice they had.

The big man frowned, piggish eyes piercing into Max's head.

"Exploration crew? I thought that was canceled."

"Oh, didn't you hear? It was reinstated at the last minute," Max said, feigning sheepishness. "Wow, this is really embarrassing. I guess we're really putting you out, aren't we?"

The man rolled his small eyes. "Everybody puts me out," he grumbled.

Max found this entirely believable. The man's demeanor was one of complete misanthropy, and while Max had his own moments during which he disliked a vast swath of humanity, this man's level of general distaste was palpable and borderline sinister.

The man was still staring hard at Max. "Who did you say you were?"

"Well, I didn't say exactly," Max said. "But my name is Maxwell Barnes. This is Axel Morales and this is—"

"Barnes?" the man interrupted. "Any relation to Professor Anderson Barnes?"

"Yeah," Max said. "That's my dad."

Max and his father had had more than their share of disagreements and tension over the years, and it ground Max's gears to rely on his father's reputation and influence at this very moment. But again, he didn't see what choice they had. He certainly would not let his own personal pride endanger either himself or his friends.

"Your dad, huh?" the man said, his tone calculating.

"That's right," Max said casually. "Know him?"

The big man grunted. "Not exactly, but his name shows up a lot on the requisition requests."

"Requisition? So he's influential in providing the ongoing funding for this research station?"

"I guess you could say that," the man admitted. "What of it?"

"Well," Max went on, girding his loins to eat a year's worth of humble pie. "I don't want to brag, but my dad kind of thinks I'm the bee's knees. And he'd be pretty upset if he found out his pet project wasn't ... you know, being all that welcoming."

The big man stood there, iron-faced, obviously weighing his options. Max could almost see the man's mind turning things over. He could either call Max's bluff, throw them all out of camp, or take their word for it and back down. Of course, if he contacted the professor, that would be tantamount to admitting he doubted the man's son. And if what Max had said was true, that might be enough to anger Professor Barnes, in turn endangering funding.

The big man finally shrugged.

"I'll give him a call on the sat radio later," he said, apparently deciding to punt the ball for now. "I guess you can come into the camp. I'll get you set up in some tents."

He turned and walked away, clearly expecting everyone to follow. Max took the opportunity to cast a victorious glance back at Axel and Isabel. Isabel gave him a thumbs up, and Axel merely shook his head in disbelief. He moved closer to Max as they followed their less-than-congenial host.

"I'm sure the Prof will be very interested to know how close you have become all of a sudden," Axel said.

"Hey, what was I supposed to do?" Max defended himself. "I'm pretty sure that guy was looking for any excuse to shoot us."

"Probably a good thing I'm on your side," Axel said. "Frankly, I don't trust him. He has tiny eyes."

"He has a tiny what?" Isabel asked, catching up with the two men.

"Eyes," Max said. "He has tiny eyes that look like a pig's."

"Oh," Isabel said, giving a quick nod. "That is true. I was thinking he might have tiny something else and is attempting to compensate with giant rifle."

"That could be too," Max said, smirking. "He does seem to have unusually small feet for a man his size."

They had arrived at the left side of the encampment, where a trio of tents were set up.

"We set these up when we thought you were still coming," the man said. "And we just never took them down. Guess that worked out, huh?"

"I guess it did," Max said. "Thanks. Does it matter who takes which?"

"Nope," the big man said. "And sorry, but we didn't set up a tent for him." He pointed at Ruo.

"That's okay," Max said. "He can bunk with me for now. I don't think Axel would have room; these tents aren't all that large."

Their host looked over at Isabel and leered. "And I guess he wouldn't be so lucky as to bunk with her."

Isabel's face tightened, and Max almost hoped she was

about to go all, well, Isabel on the man. As if possible, the man's eyes grew smaller as he observed the gorgeous woman, and gleamed with lust.

Axel leaned over and muttered into Max's ear, "You're going to have trouble with this one."

This time, Max entirely agreed.

8

The big man's name was Kane, although he did not deign to tell anyone if that was his first name or last. Either way, it was a single syllable word, and that was about all he uttered for the rest of the encounter. He showed the newcomers around the rest of the camp, mostly pointing out the salient details with a finger stab and a grunt. Max learned the smaller building Kane had exited when they first arrived was the radio hut, and the larger building was the communal dining hall.

After dumping the gear into their respective tents, they had convened in the hall and now huddled together at one end of the central table, commiserating in low tones.

The rustic dining hall was a large, open room with a high ceiling supported by thick wooden beams. The walls were made of rough-hewn logs, and the floors covered in a layer of sawdust, which Max assumed was replaced every so often—it appeared due for a changing. A massive stone fireplace occupied one end of the room, its chimney reaching up to the rafters. Down the center of the room ran a long table with benches on either side. The table was scarred and worn, the result of years of use by the researchers and staff who called the basecamp home. At the opposite end of the room, there was a large wooden counter where food was served. The light was dim, filtered through small windows high up on the walls, casting long shadows across the room.

There were two other men in the place, and one woman, none of whom looked any friendlier than Kane. They had all exchanged mumbled greetings, but no one seemed eager to deepen these superficial relationships. The air in the place was stale and overly warm, and Max longed to step back outside where it was cool.

"Is it just me, or are we not welcome here?" Max said. The question was purely rhetorical, for the answer was obvious. Their arrival was neither expected nor wanted.

"Do you think Kane will call in to the Professor?" Axel asked.

Max shrugged. "I don't know. If he does, we're sunk."

"He might not realize that's what he's doing," Axel pointed out. "I mean, if Kane just radios in and asks the simple question, the Prof might not understand exactly what he's answering."

"Then maybe we should pull a little trick from our childhood," Max suggested, a small grin playing across his handsome face.

Axel looked at his friend, momentarily confused, and then light dawned and he chuckled. "You mean the whole 'throw yourself on the Prof's mercy' thing?"

Max nodded.

Isabel raised an eyebrow. "I think there is story to be told."

"There always is," Max said. "Only in this case, it's not likely to make you angry, as opposed to pretty much all the others we tell you."

"Then let us hear it," she prompted.

Axel took the lead. "When we were kids, we would always try to be the first one to tell on ourselves to the Prof, because we discovered that whoever broke the bad news first got the benefit of the doubt."

"Not to mention that whoever tells the story gets to frame the narrative," Max added.

"Exactly," Axel said. "Which is why I think you should call up the Professor first and let him know exactly what's going on. Better he hears it from you than Kane."

Max was about to voice agreement when the door burst open, letting in a much-welcomed breeze of fresh mountain air.

"Hey, folks!" said a cheery voice.

All the newcomers turned to look, but Max noticed the three regulars didn't even bother to glance around.

The door slammed shut with a resounding thud, causing Max to turn his attention toward the man who had just entered the room. He was a tall, slender figure, his limbs seeming too long for his body. His hair was a pale blonde, messy and unkempt, with strands sticking out from under the knitted beanie that was pulled low on his forehead. A scruffy growth of stubble covered his chin, giving him a rugged and unshaven appearance. The man's face was lit up with a huge grin, curling his lips into a wide smile as he scanned the room and caught sight of Max and the others. The expression on his face brightened even further, and he made a beeline toward them, his strides quickly closing the distance.

"Hey, new blood!" He stuck out his hand and gave everyone a hearty shake. "I thought you all weren't coming!"

"Change of plans," Max said hurriedly. "My name's Max."

"Call me Dog. Who're your friends?"

"Dog?"

The man laughed and nodded. "Not my real name, of course, but that's what I go by around here."

Max introduced the others, and a round of greetings were exchanged.

Dog sat down next to them without invitation and launched into a detailed monologue about the camp. Even though this lecture was not elicited, Max found it informative and entertaining. Dog had a pleasant and energetic style, and it was certainly nice to finally meet someone who didn't appear to wish them dead.

"So that's about it," Dog concluded. "If you have any questions, just ask the Dog. I've got all the answers. I mean, they might not be the correct answers, but you can't have everything!"

He burst into laughter, and the others joined in politely.

Max found the man intriguing. He appeared happy and untroubled, but Max thought he detected an undercurrent of something that ran opposed to outward appearances. Max wondered about the man's nickname, "Dog," and whether he'd chosen it himself or had it slapped on by a less-than-charitable source.

Dog checked his watch. "Hey, we've got about an hour before feeding time. You folks wanna play horseshoes? The pits are clear of snow."

"Dog, shut up," one of the other men groused from the far end of the table. "No one wants to play your damn game."

Dog's face fell like a child being told he couldn't have a sucker.

"We'd love to play," Max said, grinning. And he meant it. He was terrible at horseshoes, but some R & R sounded just perfect to him.

"Oh, how adorable," the same man said, rolling his eyes. "Dog's found a little buddy."

Axel's face flushed at the remark, but Max caught his eye and shook his head.

The five of them rose as one and headed for the door, studiously avoiding the other sullen camp members.

"Yeah," the woman piped up. "Dog's got three puppies and one bitch."

It happened so fast Max didn't have a chance of stopping it. His eyes widened in shock as Isabel moved with lightning speed across the room, her lithe form launching onto the table. In one fluid motion, she planted a foot on the chest of the other woman, using her as a human surfboard. The two figures collided with a deafening crash, the back of the woman's chair splintering under the impact. Max's pulse raced as he caught a glimpse of metal glinting in the dim light, realizing with a jolt Isabel's opponent had pulled out a knife.

"Isabel! Watch out!"

He needn't have bothered speaking, for Isabel had produced her own weapon—the knife she had purchased in Lhasa. Isabel had used such a weapon to claim many victims, and Max couldn't help but feel sorry for the other woman who was about to face its sharpened edge. Isabel and her foe locked in a fierce battle, each matching the other in strength and skill. They broke apart and backed into the center of the room, as the onlookers retreated to the walls, giving the fighters ample space to engage in their deadly dance. Max fought against his own instinct to rush in and assist.

"Don't you dare," Axel muttered, reading Max's mind. "If you go in there to save her, she will never forgive you. She wants to do this on her own."

Max knew Axel was right, but his heart was in his throat as the two women made for each other again, both knives glinting in the light coming in through the windows. Isabel crouched low, her eyes never leaving the other woman's face, trying to anticipate her next move. The other woman did much the same, but Max started to notice a hint of uncertainty. No doubt she had expected Isabel to be an easy mark. Otherwise, she probably would never have made the snarky comment.

Isabel charged.

The two women clinched, clutching each other's knife hands with iron grips.

"Come on, Grits," one of the two men yelled. "She

doesn't look so tough. Give her a good poke with your knife. That'll settle her down."

Grits? Max sent the man a glare, but held his ground.

Both women hit the floor once more, knives flashing, grunts sounding. If Max hadn't been so concerned for Isabel's welfare, he might've enjoyed watching the struggle. Both women were athletic and skilled.

"You're not actually worried about her, are you?" Axel whispered.

Max shrugged. "Aren't you?"

"Not even a little. You've seen her fight."

Max grimaced. "Yeah, I know. But there's always a faster gun, right? Or in this case, a sharper knife."

At first, Max couldn't believe what he was hearing, but then he looked up at Axel's face and confirmed that his friend was actually chuckling.

"Are you nuts?" Max asked. "Isabel's on the verge of getting sliced open!"

"First, she's going to be fine. She's going to win this. Second, you know as well as I do you're just worried because you care so much."

"Oh, shut up," Max said, but he couldn't deny his friend's words.

And then, as if in direct compliance with Axel's prediction, Isabel flipped her opponent onto her back and pinned her there, holding her knife tight against the other woman's throbbing throat.

"What is this you said to me?" Isabel asked fiercely.

"I said you're a—"

The door burst open.

"What the hell is going on in here?" Kane demanded, charging inside like a grizzly bear with an abscessed tooth. "I said no fighting in camp. If you want to fight, go out into the wilderness so when you kill yourselves, the wild animals can eat you. Don't make me bury you or do any damn paperwork!"

Slowly and reluctantly, Isabell removed her knife from the woman's throat. Even more reluctantly, she drew back and stood up, allowing her opponent to get to her feet.

"I'm not even going to ask what this was about," Kane said. "Because frankly, I don't care. Get back to your business, leave each other alone, and stop bothering me with all these problems!" With a final oath, Kane turned on his heel, stomped from the room, and slammed the door behind him.

There were a few moments of uncomfortable silence, which was suddenly broken by an overly cheerful voice chirping,

"So, you're all still down for horseshoes, right?"

~

THEY WERE, as it turned out, still down for horseshoes. Dog and Isabel teamed up against Axel and Max, with Ruo trading sides, and before long laughter and good-natured trash talking punctuated the crisp air of the camp. Max reveled in the experience. Even though they were still at the base of the mountains, he felt on top of the world. Whether or not it was the positive effects of the chang, he and the others had thus far experienced little altitude sickness—although the real test would be during their first climb.

As the dinner bell rang, Dog and Isabel had completely crushed their opponents. As the group walked to the dining hall, Max reached out and clapped Dog on the back.

"Good grief, man," he said. "What are you, some sort of horseshoe world champion?"

Dog laughed. "No, I just have a lot of time to practice. And because nobody around here will ever play with me, I get to be both teams."

Everyone chuckled, but Max didn't miss the note of sadness in the man's voice. It was clear he found life at the camp lonely, and he wondered why Dog seemed to be something of an outcast. What did everyone else have against him?

Dinner was basic: MREs with some canned vegetables on the side. The sketchy rations caused Max to remember the delicious meal he and the others had in Lhasa, but he cheered slightly when Dog went into the back and returned with several cans of chang.

"You ever had this?" Dog asked, holding up the cans.

"For the first time in Lhasa," Axel said. "Right near the top of my list."

"Why are you giving the chang to the newbies?" one of the other men grumbled. "We're running low as it is."

"Call it hospitality, Fitch," Dog replied. "But I suppose you've never heard of it."

Dog said this, as he had said everything else since their arrival, with a good-natured and almost self-deprecating manner, but Max detected an edge in his voice when he spoke to the man named Fitch.

"It's okay," Max said, waving his hand carelessly. "If it's going to cause a problem, we won't have any."

"It's no problem," Dog said.

"Yeah, it *is* a problem." Fitch stood up from the table.

"Sit down," Kane said, not glancing up from his MRE.

Fitch turned toward the bigger man, scowling fiercely. "But boss, we're almost out of chang. We aren't going back into town for some time yet."

"I said, sit down!" Kane roared, half-rising from his chair. "There's a supply van coming in later. Besides, do you know who this guy is?"

Silence.

"It's Anderson Barnes' kid. You mess with him and we might all end up headed home. You think that's worth a couple cans of chang?"

No answer.

"Well, do ya!"

"No, Kane."

"Good. Then sit down and shut up. You get thirsty, there's a bottle of crap vodka under the desk in the radio room."

Dog's face twisted into a comical, knotted expression as he struggled to keep his mirth under wraps. He passed out cans of chang to Max, Axel, Isabel, and Ruo. He kept the last one for himself and then took a seat, popping the top of the can. He took a long swig and then looked over at Max.

"I don't think I've ever seen anything like that," he said,

keeping his voice low. "Kane usually lets Fitch do pretty much whatever he wants."

"And you?" Axel asked.

"I am a different story," Dog said, his mood darkening.

"I've noticed there seems to be something between you and the others," Max ventured. "Care to fill us in why?"

Dog hesitated, taking another drink and looking out one of the building's windows at the sun that was beginning its westward descent. "It's not something I'm proud of," he said. "And that's kind of why I have put up with it so long. I guess I kind of feel like I deserve it."

"What are you talking about? The treatment or the nickname?" Max asked.

"Both, I guess," Dog said.

"I can't imagine what you could've done to deserve all of this," Axel said. "Just the little I've seen was enough to set me on edge. How have you stood it?"

"I haven't had a lot of choice, I guess. And, like I said, at first it seemed like just desserts. And by the time I was having second thoughts about that, it had been going on so long it just seemed sort of normal."

"Why don't you just tell us the story, then," Axel prompted gently.

Dog finished off his can and smashed it by slamming it against the table top. He picked up the crushed aluminum and tossed it into the nearest bin with a practiced shot. Then he started to talk.

"It was not long before I came out here," he began. "Well, a year ago. About a month after I arrived, a group headed up into the mountains. Of course, I wanted to go along, never having been before, and so I pestered the others until they finally agreed just to shut me up. I was trouble right from the beginning, and they probably should've sent me back. I did several stupid things, but they were only inconvenient mistakes, nothing that could harm or kill anyone. On the third day of the outing, a stiff wind came up and sealed off the pass we used on the way up, forcing us to find an alternate route. Unfortunately, the only one we could find was across a narrow crevasse. We used a rope and managed to swing to the other side, and secured that end of the rope so the heavier members of the party could cross. I made it just fine, but then another member of the group, Dante, decided he would go next."

"Dante?" Max asked. He looked around the room as if he might see the aforementioned Dante sitting in a place he hadn't noticed yet.

"Dante isn't with the camp anymore," Dog said with grim finality. "When he started across the ropes, one of the metal stakes pulled free. Instinctively, I grabbed it and the trailing rope pulled me over the edge of the crevasse. Dante and I hung there, looking down into a ravine that just never seemed to end. With the wind blowing the snow, I couldn't even see the bottom. We looked at each other, and I could see he was terrified. I was scared too. And then they started yelling from above us, telling us the rope was breaking. I followed where they were pointing and saw the weak point in the rope. It was on Dante's side, and fraying quickly."

Dog paused, and his hand reached out as if searching for his beer. Without saying a word, Axel pushed his unfinished can into Dog's unconsciously grasping fingers. The man drained it, crushed it, and tossed it. Then he continued.

"I can't even describe his face. It had every emotion, all at once. But his eyes, though terrified, were also kind when he looked right at me—right into my soul—and said, 'Cut the rope, Davey. Cut the rope. That'll lighten the load, and you'll survive.'"

The entire room was silent, listening, even though half those in attendance already knew the story—had experienced it firsthand.

Dog—Davey—swallowed hard, forcing back his growing emotions. "But I couldn't do it. I couldn't cut it. I even took my knife out, but I couldn't go through with it. Dante understood what was happening inside me, so he ... well, he spared me the trouble. He pulled out his own knife and cut the rope."

There was a long pause, during which the only sound was the occasional pop and crackle of a burning log in the fireplace.

"I can still see his body drop away, growing fainter as it disappeared into the gusting snow. It didn't look like he was falling, though; it just looked like he grew smaller and transparent. And then he was gone."

Dog stopped speaking, and it was clear he was finished with his tale. There was a muttered oath from Fitch and a rush of exhales from Max and the others who'd been holding their collective breath.

"That's quite a story," Max said, feeling like an idiot for making such an obvious statement, but what else was there to say? "Sounds like Dante knew there was no other choice. It was probably him or both of you, right?"

Dog shrugged. "I suppose."

"I suppose nothing!" Fitch exploded. He jumped up from his chair, almost sending it flying, and stormed his way across the room. The other people in the room stiffened in anticipation, not knowing what would happen next. Fitch started to pace back and forth, rage radiating from his body. He was so angry his face was red, and he was almost frothing at the mouth as he shouted and spat out words. "We were all watching—it sure looked to me like Dante reached out to grab your arm and you cut first!"

"That's a damn lie!" Dog was on his feet now, his own face flushed and his eyes filling with tears. "How could you have seen anything, it was blowing snow all over the place —we were hanging down in the crevasse—"

"Oh, we saw," Fitch said, his voice dropping almost to a whisper that was anything but soothing.

He moved closer, and then he and Dog were face to face. Dog was a hair taller, but Fitch was broader and thicker. Unless the thinner man was adept at martial arts, he'd be bested in an altercation, because he'd not survive a fight where weight and brute strength made the difference. Max glanced at the others, trying to read their intent; he was uncertain whether or not to step in, knowing this was technically none of their concern.

"We saw," Fitch repeated. "And you cut the rope. If you'd just waited, we could have saved both of you ... *Dog.*"

Well, that explains the nickname, Max thought.

Silently, Grits, along with a man Max hadn't met yet, got

up and went to stand behind Fitch. Now it was stacking up to be a real beat-down. Their concern or not, Max wasn't going to sit back and let an outnumbered man get beaten to a pulp. He leaned forward, ready to spring into action. A quick look showed him Axel and Isabel were on the same page, their bodies slightly bent, muscles tensed.

"You've gotta be kidding me." It was Kane once more. A loud screeching filled the room as he pushed back his wooden chair and stood up, towering over every other standing person. "What am I, a damn babysitter? Whatever happened, it's done. And I sure don't want you idiots getting blood all over where we eat. I also don't want to deal with any medical evacs, so whatever problems you people have, here are the rules: One, deal with them out of camp. Two, make it permanent. And three, don't let me find the body."

He reached down to the table, grabbed his cup, and drained its contents. Max didn't know what the man was drinking, but he was pretty sure it wasn't water. Then Kane slammed the cup back down, gestured at his dishes, and said,

"Someone clean that up."

Then he lumbered his way from the dining hall, leaving a trail of harsh curses and a slamming door behind him. The building shook with the force of the shutting door, and the concussive report seemed to shake the concerned parties from their rage fever. Fitch muttered something Max couldn't make out and returned to his seat, followed by Grits and the other man.

Dog stood there a few moments longer, then turned slowly and left the building.

"You think we should go after him?" Max asked.

Axel shook his head. "Nah. Let him go. Lot of moving parts in this camp, and we don't yet know which way is up."

"Indeed," Isabel agreed. "I want to believe Dog, but we do not really know what the truth is."

Max nodded. " Okay. Let's just keep our noses clean and our eyes open." He glanced around. "By the way, I wonder if there's any more chang?"

9

Later, all four gathered in Max's tent. Max sat on his cot, while the others perched on crates or cross-legged on the floor.

"So, what do you think?" Axel asked.

Max shrugged. "I think it's a shame they don't have more chang around here. No wonder the others were upset Dog was giving it away to newcomers."

"Obviously, that's not what I was talking about," Axel said. "What I mean is, there are a lot of weird things happening here."

"Yeah, I know," Max nodded. "I was thinking the same thing. There are a lot of personnel dynamics I'm not sure we should get involved with."

"Especially since I am not sure who is in the right," Isabella pointed out. "Dog is definitely the nicest, but that does not mean he is good guy."

"That's assuming there *are* traditional good guys," Axel

said, huffing. “Frankly, everyone here seems to be a bit of a roughneck.”

“I’m sure that’s been said about us, too,” Max chuckled.

Axel snorted. “Yeah, probably. But they seem to have some shady secrets and skeletons in the closet, you know?”

“I’m sure that’s been said about us, too.”

This time, Axel laughed out loud. “Okay, you got me. But you know what I mean.”

“Yeah,” Max relented. “That’s another reason I want to call my dad and try to get the inside story. I’m sure we won’t get it from any of these people.”

“Definitely not,” Isabel agreed. “So, what is plan?”

“Well, since our cell phones don’t work out here,” Max said. “I’m going to sneak into the radio building and call from there.”

“Do you know how to do that?” Isabel asked doubtfully.

Max gave an offended expression. “What are you talking about? I thought you had faith in me!”

Isabel smiled charmingly. “I have always the faith in you, especially if it involves you doing stupid things.”

“Now I definitely know what I’m doing,” Max said. “Anything to restore your confidence.”

“I will settle for some answers,” Isabel answered. “I do not like working in the dark.”

“Speaking of the dark,” Axel interrupted. “We’re just about there. If you’re planning to head to the radio, now might be a good time.”

Max nodded and stood up from the cot. He approached the tent flap and looked outside cautiously.

“It feels like we’re prisoners in our own quarters,” Max

muttered. "It's not just about not being welcomed, I think we're actively resented."

"We aren't here to make friends," Axel said, shrugging. "Let's just settle things with the professor and see what we can find out about the scroll."

"Yeah," Max agreed. "And I've got more research on my laptop I can share with Kane. By the way, I saw a solar panel on top of the dining hall and heard a generator running. Maybe I can find an outlet to charge it up."

Max suddenly jerked back into the tent.

"What is wrong?" Isabel asked.

"I saw Grits walking through the middle of the camp," Max said. "What's with all the weird names around here? Grits, Dog, Fitch?"

"I got the idea 'Dog' was insult to his lack of courage," Isabel said. "But I do not know where the name Grits would come from."

"Maybe she likes grits or she's got a lot of grit," Axel suggested.

Max moved back to the tent flap and looked outside again. This time, he didn't jump back, instead opening the flap a little wider.

"Okay," he whispered. "It looks clear, and it's dark enough. The sun is setting behind the mountains, creating some nice, convenient shadows."

"Are you sure you don't want me to go?" Axel asked.

Max gave him a look. "You? You'll stick out like one of those mountains. No, I think someone normal-sized should make the attempt. From a stealth perspective, Isabel might even be better, but she wouldn't be able to pull the Barnes rank. That might be the only way to get the professor on the line."

Max stuck his head out of the tent and looked left and right.

No one in sight.

He turned back to the others. "After I leave, Axel and Isabel should go back to their tents. Ruo, if you're tired of the ground, you can sleep in my cot tonight."

Ruo gratefully claimed the cot, while the others nodded in agreement and followed Max outside.

As he walked through the camp, Max heard the distant hum of the generator and the overhead screech of a Himalayan Golden Eagle. The shadows had fallen heavy over the valley and clutched at the camp like dark fingers. Max felt a shiver up his back, but ignored it and moved to hide behind a stack of crates. The communications hut was near the center of the camp, making it difficult to reach unobserved. As he prepared to step out from the crates, he heard a cheerful whistle and saw Dog walking by with a rifle over his shoulder.

Interesting, Max thought. *Apparently, they take security seriously around here.*

He flattened against the crates, his back pressing painfully into the wood. He didn't think Dog was an enemy, but he didn't trust anyone. He couldn't afford to. He held his breath as Dog drew nearer, the whistling becoming more irritating.

Nobody likes a whistler. Now turn around and move on.

Almost as if listening, Dog did exactly that, stopping his forward progress, checking his watch, and then making an abrupt about face. He headed toward the opposite end of the camp, still whistling, still ambling, still being quintessentially Dog. The man was easygoing and congenial enough, but that could all be a front.

As the sounds of whistling and Dog's footsteps faded into the distance, Max made his next move. Even in this short period, the darkness had deepened, and Max felt a little better about his chances. He moved to the next point of concealment, which was a trio of metal barrels, probably containing diesel fuel for the generator. Max made a mental note to check out the location of the generator and find out which areas of the camp were wired for electricity. He made it to the barrels without problem and hesitated for just a few seconds before making his next move. He wasn't sure which would be better: continuing his crab-like progress or simply walking nonchalantly toward the radio room. Certainly, his current strategy made him infinitely more suspicious looking, but if he tried the casual approach and got caught—which he almost assuredly would be—the game would be over.

Better to play it safe. Surely if I can sneak through the jungle, I can sneak through a darkened campsite.

The radio hut was now within sight. Its windows were dark, and as he approached from this new angle, he saw wires leading to it from around the rear of the dining hall.

Presumably, that's where the generator is located.

This final stretch was far too open for his liking, probably a strategic choice. If the perimeter of the camp was breached, one would not want to provide cover for the enemy all the way to the camp's most important asset, a sound strategy that was proving highly annoying in this case. Max did not consider himself the enemy, of course, but the precautions were having the identical effect.

Even though it wasn't terribly far from the barrels to the radio hut, it felt like the length of a football field as Max made his way through the ever-dimming light, every moment expecting to hear an arresting shout or, much worse, a bellowing gunshot and a sharp thud against his back.

But neither of those things happened. Max reached the door safely and placed his hand on the handle. He gave it a slight rattle, trying not to make too much noise.

And his heart sank as he discovered it was locked.

As he bent to look at the mechanism, however, he realized it was of the most simple variety. Sticking in his hand in his pocket, he came out with his Swiss Army knife and extended the smaller blade. He stuck the blade into the key slot and jiggled it around until he found the correct tension point. After applying just the right amount of pressure, a satisfying click signaled success, and he smiled. He gripped the knob again, gave it a turn, and this time the door swung open.

Max grimaced as the hinges squealed in protest, and he cursed whoever was tasked with working maintenance for the camp; they were definitely falling down on the job. Instinctively, he felt around for a light switch, but then caught himself. There was a window in the hut, and having it ablaze with light would certainly alert everyone in sight. Instead, he waited for a moment, letting his eyes adjust to the darkness. Then he reached into his pocket, withdrew his cell phone, and activated the flashlight app. As he did, the phone alerted him to low battery, and he grunted. His laptop wasn't the only thing he needed to charge. Hopefully, it would last long enough for him to get a good sense of the available equipment.

He played the phone's beam over his surroundings, revealing a table upon which sat an array of communications equipment, with a single chair in front. Sat radio communication was not one of Max's specialties, but he hoped he could figure this one out, as it did not appear to be a particularly advanced model. He had used small satellite phones, like the one that had been in the luggage they'd lost in Shanghai, but this was entirely different. A moment later, however, he was gratified to discover a list of instructions pinned to a 2x4 above the device. He saw his father's name listed and to the right in parentheses was the word, "Groundhog."

Groundhog? Max thought. *Codename?*

If so, why would his father allow himself to be saddled with a codename as stupid as Groundhog?

Nevertheless, after reading the instructions, Max felt reasonably confident he could make contact, assuming the equipment worked as intended. As a precaution, he used his phone to photograph the cheat sheet, and then turned back to the chair. He was just about to sit down at the table and try his hand when he heard a heavy boot crunch on the gravel outside the door.

"You lost, Barnes?"

Kane.

Despite himself, Max started, whipping around to see

the door completely blotted out by the big man's frame. His heart pounded, and a bead of sweat popped out on the side of his forehead and trickled down. He hoped fervently Kane couldn't see how nervous he was in the darkness.

"Oh! Hey! Fancy seeing you here."

"You lost?" Kane repeated, ignoring Max's initial reaction.

"No, not lost," Max said, hoping his voice didn't tremble. "I was just checking out more of the camp's facilities, and didn't want to bother anybody to ask for a tour. Especially this late at night."

"How thoughtful of you," Kane said, his voice rumbling low with sarcasm. "Believe it or not, though, we take security at the camp pretty seriously. You're wandering around in the dark and liable to get yourself shot by one of our over-vigilant camp sentries."

"Well, I'm sure my father will be happy to hear the university's employees are taking their responsibilities so seriously," Max said meaningfully. He couldn't tell for sure in the dark, but he thought Kane's eyes narrowed a bit at the word "employees."

Don't push it too far, Max told himself.

"Is that what you were planning to do?" Kane asked. "Call your daddy?"

Max thought fast; was it better to admit his true intention or deny it all together? What would Kane make of Max's intention to contact his father? Was the man smart enough to divine Max's real purpose or would he merely assume Max wanted to touch base with his old man? Max had no reason to think the big man knew anything about his often contentious relationship with his father, so he decided to assume the persona of a dutiful son checking in with good old pops.

"I just wanted to let my dad know we arrived. Our cell phones don't seem to be working out here, and our sat phone was in the luggage we lost." He laughed and bopped himself on the side of the head. "Silly me, right? As many times as I have been in inaccessible locations around the world, you'd think I would know to bring a spare by now. Ha!"

"Yes," Kane said slowly. "Very silly indeed." He stood there, unmoving, and observed Max for a time long enough to make the situation awkward. "Well, I'm sorry to tell you only approved individuals are allowed to use the radio equipment."

"Sure, no problem," Max said. "I am willing to do whatever it takes to become approved."

"That's just the thing," Kane said, making a rather lazy attempt to sound regretful. "We can only have a certain number of people on the approved list at a time. And I'm afraid it's all full at the moment. Until someone else drops off, we can't even *begin* the process of getting you approved. Expensive stuff, this equipment. Takes some instruction and knowledge. One doesn't just sit down and use it. You understand, I'm sure ... don't you?"

"Oh, yeah," Max said, waving his hand carelessly. "Totally fine."

"Of course," Kane hastened to add. "If you want to write out a message, I'll have one of the approved radio operators send it for you. That way, you can get your message out, but we won't be breaking any important regulations."

"Sounds good," Max said. Another awkward silence ensued until Kane finally said,

"Anything else? You need an escort to the privy?"

"No," Max said, shaking his head. "I think I'll just head back to my tent."

"I think that's a really good idea."

Kane stepped back and to the side to let Max exit the small building, which Max reluctantly did. No words were exchanged as Max slowly walked away, glancing back once to see if Kane was watching. But the big man seemed to be paying no attention whatsoever, instead holding a penlight with one hand and examining the lock on the door.

Max groaned. He had used his knife blade in semi-darkness, which almost certainly meant he'd left minute scratch marks, something Kane would definitely notice.

When he reached the stack of crates, he looked back again, but now Kane was out of sight and the light was on in the building.

Max swore. *No hope of sneaking back there right now.*

Just then, he heard what sounded like the popping top of a soda can coming from somewhere deeper in the camp. Instead of going back to his tent, he took advantage of whatever was preoccupying Kane's attention and cut back around in a wide berth, heading toward where he'd heard the sound. As he crossed behind the radio hut, he saw there was also a light on in the dining hall, near the back where the kitchen was located.

He drew nearer and, as he did, heard mumbling voices.

I can hear them, he thought curiously.

But a little farther on, he understood why—the window on the side of the building was propped open, no doubt letting in a bit of fresh, albeit cold, outside air. Max imagined it could get quite warm in the back of the kitchen, especially during cleanup.

Keeping his head on a swivel, Max moved closer to the building until he was crouched directly beneath the window.

He had to move carefully and slowly to avoid the same crunch of rock that had alerted him to Kane's appearance.

He held still, listening, and now was sure there were two voices: one man and one woman. Most of the windows of the hall were set high, but the one in the kitchen was lower. As they continued speaking, Max reached upward to the sill with both hands, and gradually pulled himself up to peer inside

Dog and Grits stood in the kitchen, each leaning against an opposite counter, drinking from cans.

Dammit, Max thought. *They* did *have more chang.*

Even with the quiet surroundings and open window, it was difficult to make out distinct words, for the two team members were speaking softly.

Max closed his eyes and tried to concentrate, but he could hear little until Dog shifted his position and moved closer to the window.

"That's just not the way it was," he said. "I don't know how many times I have to go over this."

If Max hadn't seen Dog's face, he might not have believed it was him speaking, for the man's voice lacked the lightheartedness from before and had assumed a hard edge Max wouldn't have thought possible.

Grits answered him, but she was still too far from the window to be understood.

Max thought he heard the name Fitch, but he couldn't be sure. He was just trying to decide if hauling himself higher on the windowsill would be worth the risk, when he heard the now familiar crunch of boots on gravel approaching from the far side of the radio hut. He let go of the sill entirely and sank down into the deep shadow surrounding the base of the dining hall.

A gigantic figure loomed in the late evening darkness, undoubtedly Kane. Max had been so engrossed in attempting to overhear the conversation between Dog and Grits that he had not heard the door of the hut open or close. The crunching boots steps halted, and Kane seemed to be fiddling with his shirt pocket. Max couldn't quite see through the gloom enough to tell what the man was doing until he heard a lighter strike and watched Kane's face light up in the glow of a torch lighter. Seconds later, he smelled the pungent odor of a cigar.

Having lit his stogie, Kane continued on his path, which led him past the dining hall and toward the far side of the camp. Max raised his head again to listen at the window, but now all was still.

Then the kitchen light flicked off.

Whether Dog and Grits had finished their conversation or had also heard Kane's footsteps was not clear; all Max knew was three people were on the move and he no longer knew exactly where any of them were.

Heart thumping, Max again went down into a low crouch and listened intently.

No sound.

He considered having another go at the radio, but decided he had taken enough risks for the night. If he was caught a second time attempting to infiltrate the communications hut, there was no telling what might happen. Even Max's connection to Professor Barnes might not be enough to save him, depending on how high Kane considered the stakes to be.

Taking his time and pre-judging every step, Max made his way back to his tent. He hesitated, his hand on the flap, and took one last opportunity to listen to the night around him. But nothing sounded out of the ordinary, so he pulled back the tent flap and stepped inside.

Suddenly realizing how tired he actually was, now that the adrenaline was seeping from his body, Max stumbled in the dark toward his cot. Turning, he sat down heavily, but then came up with a yelp as he realized he had sat down on someone.

Ruo!

He had forgotten he had told the little man to use the cot tonight. Max groaned inwardly, but wasn't about to ask him to move. Pulling out his cellphone, he once more activated the flashlight app, hoping against hope it had just enough battery life to see exactly where Ruo had unrolled the sleeping bag. As he rotated the light, he caught sight of something dark on his hands.

Peering closer, he chilled as he realized his hands were covered in blood.

10

"I don't have to tell you how disappointed I am," Kane said, striding up and down the center of the dining hall with his hands clasped behind his back. "I gave you specific instructions to take your shenanigans out of camp. And what do you do? You go and kill someone in a tent—and not *just* anyone, but a damn visitor! Does anyone want to venture a guess as to why I might be upset about this?" Silence filled the room as Kane came to an abrupt halt and stood like a statue, only his eyes moving as he glared at each person individually. "No one? Don't make me start calling names."

Dog raised his hand and asked, "Because we don't want to lose our funding?"

"Oh look, the dog barks," Fitch snickered.

Twin snorts escaped both Grits and the other man whose name Max still hadn't discovered.

"Shut up!" Kane roared. "You guys are really this stupid?

We've got to stop this infighting right now or someone else is going to end up dead and we won't be able to cover it up."

Max raised his hand, an inquisitive expression on his face. "Are you suggesting we should cover *this* up?"

"Are you suggesting we should report it?"

"I sort of assumed we would. Isn't that standard operating procedure?"

"I think I would know more about the SOP around here than you," Kane said. "Or are you going to pretend that just because you're Professor Barnes' golden son, you know better than anyone?"

"Not at all," Max said, shrugging. "It's just it doesn't take a genius to know that whenever someone dies, it's usually a big deal."

"New rules out here, Professor Junior. First, none of you are even supposed to be here. Second, the guy who died wasn't supposed to be part of the expedition, even when it was approved."

"Okay," Axel said. "A couple of things of my own." He stood up from his chair as he spoke, and Max couldn't help but compare the men's sizes. It was almost a one-to-one ratio, with Axel possibly edging out Kane in breadth of shoulder. "Do you even know the guy's name?" He looked around the room questioningly, but no one answered. "In case you don't, it was Ruo. I didn't know much about him, but he seemed like a decent guy. Second of all, are you telling me that even when the three of us *were* expected, Ruo wasn't part of it?"

"Not that it has to do with anything," Kane grumbled. "But no. Why do you think we didn't have a tent ready for the little fella?" The big man began pacing again and as he turned to walk in the other direction, Max saw his intertwined fingers were white from the strength of his grip. "Now, let's get back to business. Here's what we're going to do about ... what was his name?" He turned to look at Axel. "Rudolph?"

"Ruo," Axel corrected.

"Here's what we're gonna do about that guy. We're going to take him with us on our next climb. Once we get to the first crevasse, over he goes. Any questions?"

Max and his two friends sat there in stunned silence. Everyone else, including Dog, simply nodded in understanding. Axel, who had never resumed his seat, looked around in amazement.

"Are you serious? We're just going to dump him into a mountain crevasse without telling anyone? What about his family? Employer? The Chinese government?"

"And there you go answering your own question," Kane said with a patronizing smile. "Do you have any idea what would happen once we started spreading the news of a dead Chinese man on this research site?"

"No, not really," Axel admitted. "Why don't you enlighten me?"

"We would likely receive an unpleasant visit from a secret branch of the Chinese military." Max was about to say something, but Kane silenced him with an outstretched hand. "And don't bring up the ol' autonomous argument, because the Chinese can do whatever they want out here. Our operations have been hanging by a thread for a year, and this accident would be the end of it."

"Accident?" Isabel said. "I do not think this was an accident. I saw the body."

"And yet, that's exactly what happened," Kane said, leaning toward Isabel. "The best-case scenario is no one finds out about Rudolph's death. If they do, we say it was an accident."

"He fell into a crevasse," Fitch added with a smirk.

"Exactly," Kane agreed, re-clasping his hands behind his back. "We can't afford trouble from the Chinese government or the university. Rudolph was just a small cog in a big machine. Nobody will miss him, and there's no need to cause any more trouble than necessary. And to those who might cause trouble, let me make myself clear." With one swift movement, Kane drew a hunting knife from a sheath on his belt and sent the weapon whistling across the room, where it stuck with a loud *thwack!* in a wooden target on the far wall. The knife quivered and thrummed, sunk deep into the wood. Kane merely stood and stared at it. Then he said, "Anyone who causes unnecessary trouble will have their head replace that target." He gestured to the knife. "I hope I'm clear." He looked around the room and received various replies:

"Perfectly."

"Crystal."

"Definitely."

"Yep."

"Go to the hell." This from Isabel, thankfully unheard by Kane.

The big man appeared satisfied and crossed the hall to reclaim his blade.

"Excellent. Now listen—we leave for the mountains at first light. So I want you, you, and you—" and here Kane pointed at Max, Axel, and Isabel "—in the community hall with your research information in five. Got it?" He didn't wait for acknowledgements, but rather strode off, assuming his order would be followed.

~

"YOU HAVE TO GET TO RADIO," Isabel said as the three huddled in Axel's tent. No one wanted to spend any more time in Max's than absolutely necessary, and Max was still trying to figure out where he would sleep that night, his old, blood-soaked cot being out of the question.

Max nodded, thinking quickly. "I do agree we should check in with the Prof, no matter what the consequences might be. But how to do it is another thing. On the way back from the dining hall, I took a quick peek at the radio hut and it looks like Kane has put on a hefty padlock. I might be able to get in if I had my pack of lock picking tools, but I left those in my other suit."

"You joking?" Axel asked. "Sometimes I'm not sure if you're joking."

"Of course, I'm joking," Max said, grinning. "You know this is the only set of clothes I own."

"Can we please focus on issue?" Isabel pleaded. "We cannot let a little thing like a padlock get in our way."

"Have you seen it? It's bigger than my head."

"And it's not like we can just shoot it off," Axel said. "Given that stealth is a concern."

"Yes, and that doesn't always work like it does in the movies."

Axel thought for a moment. "What about the window?"

Max considered this and then shrugged. "I guess I don't really know. I didn't check it out when I was there, because the only thing I was concerned about was getting to the radio. I should've taken more time to inspect the rest of the hut, but I was in a bit of a hurry and didn't know Kane was lurking around. I don't think that guy ever sleeps." He tried to check his phone for the time, but discovered it was totally dead. "Speaking of Kane, I'm sure he is getting peeved to be waiting for us. Let me grab my laptop and we'll head over to the hall."

The meeting with Kane was brief and efficient. Using a power strip in the hall, Max plugged in his computer and went over some of his research with Kane—although holding some back—and they made a general plan for a climb the next day. They were not going to do the "big climb" yet. Per Kane's recommendation, they would do some preliminary exploration based on the closest data points in the research, to see if it provided any new information or leads. If so, they could gather said information and head back to basecamp to analyze, report, and plan for a larger expedition a week or so later.

The plan sounded good to Max. He knew he and the others were not accustomed to climbing, and he could only hope the transition would not be too grueling. Within half an hour, the trio of explorers were back in Axel's tent, picking up where they'd left off.

"I can tell you one thing," Axel said. "I really don't want to go on this climb without making contact with the Prof."

Max cocked an eyebrow. "You thinking there'll be hijinks? Other than surreptitiously dropping a dead body down a frozen crevasse, I mean."

"I'm a little worried about one of us being one of those dead bodies. I don't trust any of these people."

"Dog seems okay," Isabel said.

"Maybe. But I'm keeping an eye on him as well."

"Well, we certainly have to go along on the climb," Max said. "Even if they weren't intending us to. That's kinda the reason we're here. But I do agree leaving word with my dad is a good idea. Then, if they try to off us, we can let them know somebody knows where we are."

"That sounds like something women have to do every time they go on a date with a new guy," Isabel huffed. "Men, they are creeps."

"Or maybe you just have bad taste in men," Max retorted.

Isabel gave Max a searching look, and then said thoughtfully, "Maybe I do."

Axel coughed once, and then said, "Anyway, I'm thinking we go with the distraction routine. I'm pretty good at breaking things, so maybe I'll cause some loud destruction on the other side of the camp. While everybody is running over to give me hell about it, Max can see what he can do about accessing the radio."

"Sounds like the best plan we have," Max agreed. "And you're right, you're definitely really good at breaking stuff. Make it good, though. I'll probably need a few minutes."

"You'll get what you get," Axel said. "I'm a bulldozer, not a miracle worker."

~

MIRACLE WORKER OR OTHERWISE, Axel made good on his commitment to cause a distraction. And what a distraction it was. Max waited outside his tent until he heard the commotion begin. As soon as he heard people begin shouting and running around the camp, he headed for the radio hut, not bothering with trying to be sneaky or remain quiet on his feet. There was no need for that; nothing could be heard over the clinging, crashing, cacophonous noise coming from Axel's approximate location.

As he arrived at the door of the hut, complete with massive, over-compensating padlock, Max couldn't completely suppress a grin at the continuing ruckus. Reaching into his pocket, he again pulled out the Swiss Army knife, trying various combinations of the included tools to pick the lock. Unfortunately, none were sufficient to spring the mechanism.

Abandoning this effort, he went around to the side of the building and began inspecting the window. It was a little high, but could be breached as long as he could get the thing open. Running his fingers along the sill, he felt the smallest crack between that and the window frame. Using the largest blade on the knife, he stuck it into the crack and pushed along the length of the sill. Bits of plaster and dried glue came showering down as he continued prying at the window.

His shoulder quickly started aching, thanks to the uncomfortable angle and height of the window, but after a minute, he pushed at the window and felt it give about half an inch. His energy restored, he used the knife to pry up the right side of the window frame, causing a similar mini avalanche of crusted construction material.

Another push on the window, and it moved up another inch. Max knew he could simply rap smartly on the window at this point it would fall into the building, but it would also likely break on the floor, and he was hoping to accomplish his mission and leave little to no trace of his actions.

With that in mind, he raised the knife and stabbed downward on the wooden window pane, sending the knife blade deep into the worn wood. Holding onto the handle of the knife, he tapped smartly on the window, sending it the rest of the way out of its moorings. The window began falling in and down, but Max held firmly to the knife handle and the sunken blade kept the window from dropping. Reaching up, Max now grabbed the exposed side of the frame, and by turning the entire thing at an angle, managed to withdraw it from the hut. He set it safely on the ground, leaning against the side of the building. He folded the knife, shoved it into his pocket, and then gripped the windowsill with both hands and shimmied through the opening.

The interior was dark, but not nearly so dark as it had been the last time he was here, and Max had no trouble seeing as he moved toward the radio. He wanted very badly to inspect the entire room, but did not know how long Axel could keep up the distraction; even now the noise seemed to be lessening.

Once at the radio, Max immediately sat down in the chair, and stabbed his forefinger at the button marked "power." The radio came to life, illuminating a bewildering number of buttons and dials. Max looked over at the wall where the cheat sheet had been, and his heart sank as he realized ... it was gone. There was still a tiny hole in the wall where it had been tacked up.

Someone had removed it.

He knew he'd taken a photo, but his phone's battery had then rudely died. Max closed his eyes and willed his memory to produce a saved image of the cheat sheet. He certainly remembered the name ground hog, and he assumed it was a codename. Moving down the list in his memory, he began to slowly recreate the steps, aided by simple logic and the process of elimination. What he could not seem to recall, but knew had been on the list of instructions, was a call sign. He would need that to make contact, but as hard as he tried, he could not seem to dredge up the digits from his memory.

QR ... no ... QD3 ... no ...

Max let out a frustrated string of curses, and sat back in the chair forcefully, causing the rickety piece of furniture to groan ominously. The noise from outside had almost entirely ceased now, and soon the camp would be returning to normalcy.

There was not much time.

Forcing himself to remain calm, Max took a long, measured look around the room. There was a tall bin in one corner that appeared to contain a variety of tightly rolled maps. On one wall was a corkboard displaying pinned snapshots, requisition forms, and index cards containing various mundane details. Nothing that looked like a radio call sign.

Max heard shouts from outside, voices that were uncomfortably close. Of course, there was a chance no one would know he was in the hut, unless they themselves had reason to use it or they happened to walk around the side where he'd removed the window.

Max drew in a deep breath, and tried to think. As his mind churned, his eyes continued to rove about.

And then he saw it.

There, on a shelf on the opposing wall, was a leather book. The spine was embossed in faded gold, and read LOG BOOK.

Getting quickly to his feet, Max crossed to the shelf and removed it. It was indeed a logbook, although it was layered in dust and didn't appear to have been used in sometime.

Still holding out hope, Max flipped the book open to reveal aged pages lined with columns and scrawled in pencil. Turning to the very back, he saw the last entry was from ten years ago and notated a call placed to the very call sign on the missing cheat sheet. Even though Max hadn't been able to remember it himself, he knew upon seeing it that this was the one.

Ripping out the page, he closed the book quickly, the cover snapping together and sending up a cloud of dust that made him cough. He replaced the book where he'd found it and covered the distance back to the sat radio in two strides.

Dropping into the chair, he scooted to the radio and put the sheet of paper on the table before him. Grabbing up the radio mic, he held down the key and read off the call sign.

At first, there was no answer, and Max waited only a few seconds before broadcasting again. A few seconds later, his heart thudded as static came over the speaker.

"This is QH302, Basecamp. Come in."

At first, Max was tongue-tied, having no idea who he was speaking to or what he should be saying. He had no desire to let the person on the other end of the conversation know he was using the radio without permission, and being a complete novice might be a red flag. However, he had no choice, as the outside voices grew ever nearer, telling him,

Time is running out.

"Hello, QH302. I'd like to speak with Professor Anderson Barnes, please."

There was a pause of several long seconds before the radio crackled again. "Request received. Deliver the passcode."

Passcode? I didn't know I needed a passcode.

Then he said the first thing that came to his mind.

"Groundhog."

He crossed his fingers and sent up a prayer to every deity he had ever heard of and could imagine on the spot.

Another long pause ensued. And then:

"This is Groundhog."

"Dad?"

As was becoming habitual, silence stretched.

"Maxwell?"

"Yeah, it's me. Look, I don't have time to explain, and I

know you'll have a lot of questions, but we're at the basecamp and things have taken a sharp left turn, so to speak."

"You're at the basecamp? But we canceled that trip."

"Oh, really?"

"Maxwell, don't play games with me. What is going on?"

"Like I said, I don't have time to explain. I just wanted you to know that we are here and—"

There was a rattling at the door as someone began fiddling with the padlock.

"Dad, I have to go. I'll explain everything later."

"Maxwell—"

The door burst open, and once again Max found himself sitting in the shadow of Kane looming in the doorway. Only this time, the man held a shotgun in his hands. The big man opened his mouth to speak, but then his eyes tracked to the radio and the microphone held in Max's hand. Obviously deciding not to speak, he instead raised the shotgun to his hip and pointed it directly at the radio. Max launched himself backward just as the shotgun roared in the room, spitting fire and lead shot. The piece of equipment practically exploded, sending a shower of sparks all over the room.

"I told you to stay away from the damn radio!" Kane roared, pumping another shell into the chamber and sending the spent one flying. Max scrambled to his feet as Kane turned the shotgun his way.

"I don't think you have time to shoot me," Max said, pointing to the table. "Looks like you've got an electrical fire on your hands."

Kane whipped around, saw Max was telling the truth,

and started trying to douse the growing flames. Max took the opportunity to grab the window sill, hoist himself up, and slip through the opening like an otter in a water show jumping through a hula hoop. He landed hard on the ground but was up in a flash, sprinting toward his tent and yelling for Axel and Isabel as he went.

11

If ever a man appeared on the verge of exploding, Kane was that man. Max had run directly to Axel's tent, hoping to find his friends there, but only Isabel was waiting. Axel had clearly not returned from his mission of distraction.

"What has happened?" Isabel asked, standing up from the crate where she'd been sitting.

"I may have gotten caught," Max said, chagrined. "And the guy who caught me is a little upset about it."

"I am guessing it is Kane?"

"What clued you in? The way the ground is shaking under his furious stomping? That his loud bellows are causing the mountains to tremble at their very foundations?"

"You are poet when frightened."

"I'm not—"

"I will go talk to him."

"I wouldn't recommend it," Max said, reaching out a

hand to halt Isabel's progress. "I don't think gallantry is the first thing on his mind. He's so angry he's liable to just walk right over you."

At that moment, Kane's deafening shouts were met with roars that equaled or exceeded them. Max slipped past Isabel and peered out the tent flap.

"It's Axel," he whispered.

The two men were looming toward each other, their faces contorted in rage, their muscles bulging with tendons, and their eyes squinted with fury. Kane seemed like a mountain ready to burst in a volcanic eruption of anger. His chest heaved, a great bellows of fire and fury, as he balled his fists like boulders, knuckles white and veins throbbing. His arms were great oaks, while his narrow eyes, a stormy gray that spoke of battles fought and won, were mere slits as he fixed them upon Axel.

As they met in the center of the camp, both men were already covered in a sheen of sweat. Axel stood opposite Kane. His eyes, dark and dangerous, were pools of molten lava ready to spew forth destruction. His own powerful arms quivered with anticipation, and his broad chest heaved with each breath. Max had always known his friend was a large guy, but seeing him now, enlarged by anger and adrenaline, Axel Morales appeared as a Goliath of the Himalayas. If Kane was any smaller, it was by a mere fraction.

The two men circled each other like starving predators, the air between them crackling with tension, an invisible barrier charged with the weight of their shared animosity. The atmosphere was thick with the smell of sweat, testosterone, and the impending violence. Their bodies were tense, coiled springs ready to snap, as they gauged each other's movements, seeking an opening. The campsite fell into an eerie silence, as if the world was holding its breath. To Max, it was like seeing a pair of mythological titans heading into battle.

"Well, this is gonna get ugly," he muttered.

"I should put a stop to this," Isabel said. "The two little boys are going to hurt themselves."

Hearing Isabel—who was certainly fit and athletic but also about a third the size of one of the men—refer to them as "two little boys" struck Max as hilarious. He started laughing, although the expression of mirth was as much out of nerves as humor.

And then the two men came together with a mighty crash. Their arms darted out and collided with one another, left and right, like dueling swordsmen fighting for honor. Growling, they met chest to chest, muscles straining, their shirts expanding at the seams. Their eyes were narrowed, their mouths twisted into sneers. For a moment, they simply stood there, nose to nose, shouting insults and threats, demanding the other man stand down. But of course, neither was willing to do so.

Kane struck first.

He moved like a charging bull, his massive frame hurtling toward Axel with startling agility. His intention was clear: to seize his opponent and crush him to the ground. But Axel was quicker, evading with a graceful sidestep. Kane stumbled and, sensing an opening, Axel pressed his advantage. Moving with the agility of a mountain lion, his nimble footwork belying the sheer mass of his frame, he circled around Kane like a predator stalking wounded prey. As Kane struggled to regain his balance from his own failed assault, Axel lunged forward, aiming a thunderous blow at his opponent's exposed flank.

Kane let out a stifled groan and stumbled, trying to absorb the impact, but the force of the blow was too great. He shifted his weight, attempting to deflect the brunt of the attack, but the pain was unmistakable. His features contorted in agony, his ruddy face turning an even deeper shade of crimson. His beady eyes, which already resembled those of a feral hog, narrowed to slits as he glared at his opponent with unbridled fury.

Axel's gamble had paid off with a mighty strike that had momentarily thrown him off balance, but then Kane grabbed Axel's extended forearm with a vice-like grip, using the momentum to propel him forward. Drawing his leg back, he delivered a savage kick to Axel's lower back, sending him stumbling and struggling to regain his footing.

Kane wasted no time in closing in for the kill, his massive frame surging forward like a predator on the hunt. But Axel, ever the tactician, had anticipated the move and spun deftly to the left as Kane barreled towards him. With fists clenched like hammers, Axel swung with all his might, connecting with a glancing blow that landed squarely on Kane's shoulder. It was a punishing strike, but not enough to finish the fight.

As Kane rushed past, Axel seized the opportunity to strike again, deftly extending his foot and sending his opponent hurtling towards the ground. Kane landed with a thud, sending up a cloud of dust and dirt that billowed around him like a shroud.

Max glanced over at Isabel.

"Is it just me, or did the ground shake?"

"It shake," Isabel replied.

Kane was already on his hands and knees, his massive frame shuddering as he struggled to regain his footing. Axel wasted no time, moving with lightning speed as he closed in on his opponent, intent on finishing the fight. With a single fluid motion, he landed on Kane's back, wrapping his sinewy arms around the man's neck in a vice-like grip.

But Kane was not so easily subdued. With a fierce determination that matched Axel's own, he rolled onto his back, his muscled form heaving with effort as he fought to break free. With a fierce grunt, he brought his right elbow crashing down into Axel's ribs, the impact sending a sharp, stabbing pain through the other man's body.

Axel gritted his teeth, his grip on Kane's throat tightening even as the two giants tumbled across the unforgiving rocky terrain. Every movement was a struggle, a test of strength and endurance, as they battled for supremacy. But despite the pain and exhaustion, Axel refused to let go, his eyes blazing with a fierce determination to emerge victorious.

As the fight continued, the rest of the camp's occupants gathered around the perimeter, most of them cheering for Kane. Both Max and Isabel exited the tent and set up their own cheering section. Dog was the only observer who remained silent, probably unwilling to cheer for Kane and too frightened to cheer for Axel.

"Kane, you want a knife?" Fitch called out.

Max looked over and saw the man actually held the implement in question—a nasty-looking Bowie knife that gleamed in the light. The audacity of the man sent a surge of anger deep into Max. Almost without thinking, he turned on his heel and marched back to Axel's tent, heading straight to the pack that sat at the foot of his best friend's cot. Bending over, he opened the top flap, stuck his hand inside, and came out with Wei's pistol they taken from the room in Lhasa. After checking to make sure there was a round in the chamber, he stepped back outside and pointed the gun directly at Fitch's head.

"Stand down with the knife or you're done here," he said, pleased that neither his voice nor hand shook.

Fitch followed the voice and looked at Max disbelievingly. Finally, he said, "I hope you know what you're doing, kid. This is something you're not gonna be able to take back."

"I know exactly what I'm doing," Max said. "I'm bringing a gun to a knife fight. Now drop the blade or I drop you."

Fitch let out a string of the most virulent curses Max had ever heard, but he did as ordered.

Throughout this exchange, the two big men had continued their struggling. Axel maintained his tight grip around Kane's throat, but the other man was refusing to yield. His face was now purple, and the veins that once had bulged now seemed on the verge of rupture.

"Give it up, Kane," Axel commanded, his deep voice ragged with strain and exhaustion. "Give it up, or I'll put you under."

Finally, just as Axel's promise seemed on the brink of fulfillment, Kane sagged and hit the ground three times with an open palm. Slowly, carefully, on the alert for any sign of trickery, Axel loosened his grip. Then he withdrew his arms entirely, stood shakily to his feet, and stepped back to allow his vanquished foe to rise.

Even more slowly, Kane did so.

Without a word or look to anyone, he turned and staggered off toward his quarters. Gradually, the spectators also dispersed, but as Fitch began to leave, he cast one final glance at Max, pointing at his own eyes with two fingers and then turning them toward Max, telling the adventurer he would be seeing him again soon.

12

IT WAS WITH THIS ANTAGONISTIC AND SUSPICIOUS PALL OVER basecamp that Max and the others rose the next morning to prepare for their first climb. They had been awakened by a deafening electronic bleating noise coming from a siren mounted on a pole on the far northern corner of the camp. Apparently, this was known as the 'Klimb Klaxon,' a deceptively lighthearted name for a device everyone, except Kane, hated with a passion. He had personally installed and named it—a surprising demonstration of levity for him—and had resisted numerous attempts to either have it removed or disabled altogether.

When Max, along with his friends, had joined the others gathering in the center of the camp, complete with climbing gear and heavy packs, they had received a few resentful glances, but no one said anything about refusing to let them join the party. Apparently, they had assumed they would be joining them on regular climbs, given the original intent of their visit. Max was not foolish enough to believe they had turned some sort of corner in terms of their acceptance, especially not with the events of the day before, but he was happy not to have to defend himself.

Fitch was there, along with Dog and Grits, and another he couldn't recognize thanks to his heavily bundled face, but assumed was the third man he had yet to meet officially. In fact, he had yet to meet others he'd seen moving around the camp, but given the general attitude of just about everyone except Dog, he hadn't made much of an effort.

Max's eyes were still bleary from sleep, and he had not had any coffee.

"What time is it, anyway?" he grumbled.

"Around 5:00," Axel said.

He was obnoxiously alert, if not chipper, and Max suspected it might have something to do with his recent victory in battle. For Axel, and for any red-blooded male, there was nothing quite like domination in combat to improve one's outlook on life.

As they stood waiting, the door to the radio hut—which had survived the electrical fire with minimal damage—burst open, and Kane strode out. Studiously avoiding making eye contact with Axel, the big man strode to the front of the group, made an abrupt and precise about-face, and clasped his hands behind his back. Max made a mental note to perform a bit of rudimentary research on the guy as soon as he had a chance; he would lay money on him having some sort of military background.

"Everyone fall in—now!" Kane bellowed, his powerful

voice cracking through the air like a pickaxe against an ice shelf.

Everyone, Axel included, did as commanded. This was yet another thing Max admired about his friend. Many men would attempt to capitalize on their victory by showing up or humiliating their defeated opponent. But Axel was not that kind of man, and even though he had soundly beaten Kane, he also respected the chain of command. Axel was not selfish enough to bask in glory at the expense of others, and he was smart enough to understand they were embarking on a highly dangerous expedition that would require teamwork and tight cohesion of the unit. Max had his doubts certain other members of the party would be capable of such grace, but he knew if problems of personnel were to arise, Axel would not be to blame.

Kane strode to the end of the line and began a systematic inspection of each member's gear. He checked the tightness of straps and buckles, and asked specific questions about what each person was carrying, before finally moving on to the next. Max watched this procedure with interest. Kane might be big, loud, overbearing, shady, and perhaps even downright criminal, but the man obviously knew what he was doing and seemed to genuinely care about the safety of his charges.

As if reading Max's thoughts, Kane stepped back to his original place, front and center, and spoke.

"Many of you have already made several trips into the mountains, so this is becoming routine to you. Don't let it. As soon as something becomes routine, you start paying less attention; you don't even think about it. I want every action you take in preparation for and during this climb to be purposeful and every decision intentional. Think before you step, look before you climb, and measure before you jump. I don't want any accidents. Not only for the safety of the person who might be hurt, but also because any incapacitation seriously endangers the rest of the group. Don't be a fool by getting yourself hurt and then making things riskier for your teammates. Stick close together. Don't wander off on your own, even if you think you see something pertinent to the mission. Wait to mention it to others, and definitely mention it to me. Don't get greedy, don't get selfish, and for God's sake, if you start getting lightheaded, stop and take a rest. Altitude sickness can come on in a hurry; it sneaks up on you, and before you know it you're tumbling down the side of the mountain and dragging somebody else along with you. And, finally, if you've got electronics, keep them off until you need them and the batteries close to your body for warmth. Cold can sap a battery faster than you might think. Even when using cellphones, keep it in airplane mode; that'll preserve the charge."

Kane looked intently at every single face, and the silence stretched into a heavy chasm of quiet. He let the silence lengthen until everyone was on the verge of cracking. At last, he unclasped his hands and brought them together in front of him with an ear-splitting slap.

"Okay, then! I think we're all on the same page, aren't we?"

As if all present had been transformed into a single entity, they all recited, "Yes, sir."

Even though he obviously had major problems with the man, Max could not deny that he knew how to lead a group. His size and voice were intimidating, yes, but Kane also had a sort of natural charisma that all great leaders possessed. This, of course, did not make him a good and decent person, it only made him effective at getting people to do what he wanted them to do.

"At ease," Kane ordered. "We fall out in fifteen."

The organized line disbanded.

Max looked at his two friends and blew out a breath. "Well, that was something."

"The man's no joke," Axel admitted.

"You made him look like one yesterday," Max said.

"I'd never admit this to anybody else," Axel admitted ruefully, "but I had my doubts how that was actually going to go. There are some guys who look big and tough but are like marshmallows in a fight. This Kane character has a steel rod running through him. We'll need to be careful around him."

"Tough or not," Isabel said, "If he does not stop looking at me like he wants to undress me, I may have to carve him open and take steel rod out."

Max could not blame Kane for finding Isabel irresistibly appealing, but he still deeply resented the big man's attention.

"If it comes to that, I will happily cheer you on," he said.

"You would not help?" Isabel looked at him slyly through long, lowered eyelashes.

Max's heart fluttered, but he managed to flash a flirtatious smile.

"You wouldn't need me."

Isabel smirked. "I cannot decide if you are being progressive or cowardly."

"Sometimes definitions can get confusing," Max said, his grin shifting toward the mischievous. "Which, quite honestly, is highly convenient for me."

Isabel rolled her eyes and turned away, her gaze coming to rest on the rising mountain peaks ahead of them.

"Are you feeling nervous?" Max asked, moving forward to stand next to her.

"Do not be ridiculous," she said, shaking her head. "I am never nervous."

"Never?"

"Never."

"I find that hard to believe," Max said. "All you've done throughout your life and never once in the grip of nerves?"

"It is as my grandmother used to say, 'You are only allowed to worry if it will make a difference.'"

Axel chuckled. "That reminds me of the story about the spy during the Cold War who was captured by the opposing side. As he was being questioned, his captors marveled at his calm demeanor and finally asked, 'Aren't you worried?' The spy looked at them, shrugged, and said, 'Would it help?'"

"You two are real self-help gurus," Max grunted. "Me, I prefer to worry myself into a lump of quivering gel. Only then can I be sure things will work themselves out."

"Seems unnecessary," Axel said, "but that's how you've always been, and I don't expect you to change now."

"Thanks, buddy." Max reached out to clap his friend on the muscular shoulder. "That makes me feel a lot better."

Axel grimaced. "Oh, well, I certainly didn't mean for *that* to happen."

Max opened his mouth to retort, but the words were interrupted by the beeping of the security entrance at the front of the camp. They all turned to look and saw a white van with some painted Chinese characters on the side, easing beneath the still-lifting guard bar.

"Well, what do we have here?" Max wondered. "Any of you read Chinese?"

Neither of his two friends answered, and Max knew for a fact that neither of them did. He expected Kane to run forward, brandishing some sort of firearm, but instead the big man strode forward, calmly and purposefully, and waving in what was for him a friendly manner. No one else seemed overly concerned either, so Max waved Dog over. Once the tall, gangly man had sidled close enough, Max asked,

"What's the story with the van?"

"Just supplies, probably." Dog grinned widely. "You knew we were low on chang, right?"

"How could I forget," Max said. "Thanks. You ready for the climb?"

The other man's demeanor immediately shifted into negative territory.

"I'm always ready, man," he said, before abruptly turning and walking away.

The others watched him go, and then Axel said quietly,

"Seems like you touched a nerve."

"Yeah," Max nodded. "And I guess we know why, given that story of his. Who do you guys believe: him or Fitch?"

"Dog," Isabel said. "Definitely."

Axel was slower to respond. When he spoke, he said, "If I had to choose, it'd be Dog. But frankly, I don't plan to be on the other end of a rope from either of them."

13

All told, there were eight members of the climbing party, and they struck out exactly fifteen minutes after Kane had shouted "at ease." They walked out of camp single file, their steps synchronized as they moved toward the towering Himalayas, majestic peaks that jutted upward like ancient sentinels standing guard at the gates to the afterlife.

The first light of dawn had just peeked over the eastern horizon, casting an orange and pink hue across the sky. As the sun crested, its golden rays stretching out to touch the earth below and illuminated the westward mountainsides in a warm glow. The light played across the rugged terrain, defining the sharp crags and deep valleys in a brilliant display of light and shadow. Snow-capped peaks shone like diamonds, reflecting the sun's rays. The sight was truly breathtaking, nature's grand concerto, with the mountains serving as the stage, and the light serving as the conductor. For those lucky enough to witness this magical display, it was a sight they would never forget—a moment of magic that would stay with them forever.

The air was pleasantly mild, with a gentle breeze that carried with it the scent of pine and damp earth. Max heard the call of a Himalayan Golden Eagle, and he wondered if it was the same one as before. He hoped so, as that somehow provided a little twinge of security, as if the eagle would be watching over them.

As they made their way up the mountain, the temperature dropped noticeably. The chill in the air was at first invigorating. Max's heavy clothes had felt too warm in the valley and even warmer during the initial leg of the trip as his body heated from exertion, but as the mercury plummeted, his overall comfort level rose.

He glanced back now and then to check on Axel and Isabel, and could see their flushed cheeks and misting breath. There had been little idle chatter before, but now there was none, and the crunching of snow and gravel underfoot was the only sound that could be heard. They had gained altitude almost immediately upon leaving camp, and the angle of ascent had only increased the farther they went.

~

BY MID-MORNING, they had gone about as far as they could before encountering some actual climbing. The rising slope of the mountain had plateaued briefly before the face then zoomed upward toward the sky. From this vantage point, it appeared sheer, although Max knew it was not.

"Break!" Kane shouted out, having spent the entire time at the head of the group.

He held up a fist and then Max had to chuckle as the big man whipped out a whistle that hung from a chain around his neck and gave three quick chirps. It looked and sounded silly, but Max had to admit the high, sharp sound carried well in the ever-thinning mountain air.

"Cold snack and water, we don't have time to heat anything," Kane went on. "Don't eat or drink too much. Don't drop layers, and pay attention to your breathing."

After providing this list of instructions, Kane stepped away from the group, sat on a boulder, and pulled out what appeared to be a folded topographic map.

Max shrugged from his pack, dropped it heavily on the ground, and then unzipped a pocket. He withdrew a packaged energy bar and then a bottle of water, which had been kept inside thermal packaging—drinking super cold water at these temperatures wasn't the greatest idea—then, using the pack as a seat, he sat down with a groan.

"Feeling the burn?" Axel inquired, coming up next to Max. He also withdrew a food item, but chose to settle onto the ground and not his pack—likely a good idea, considering his bulk.

Max nodded. "Yep, just a little. Figured I'd be okay after our long treks in the jungle, but it's like using different muscles."

Isabel followed Max's lead with the refreshment and pack, and the trio enjoyed the respite from the exertions of constant ascent.

"Anyone feeling sickly from the altitude?"

Max looked over to see Dog approaching.

The thin man had shown little effort at keeping up his place in line. In fact, it seemed to Max he was holding back in order not to overtake Kane at the front of the line. Dog's long legs ate up the ground, even in the increasingly difficult terrain—it was as if he was built for this. Mountain climbing did not rely on brute strength; it required conditioning and endurance.

"Not yet," Max said, "but I kind of expect to. I don't have a lot of experience climbing, and I'm not so stupid as to be one of those guys who thinks they can just drop in and do someone else's job. I'm a little worried we're gonna end up slowing the rest of you down."

Dog laughed. "Oh, don't worry about that. Kane won't let that happen. If you need to rest for safety purposes, then definitely call out. But don't think you're going to escape a little razzing."

"Razzing I can handle," Max said. "It's getting tossed into a crevasse that I have a hard time dealing with." He glanced around. "Speaking of which, where's Ruo's body? I thought we were tossing him over the mountain."

Dog shrugged, but his eyes seemed to grow a bit shifty. "No idea. I guess that's something you'd have to ask Kane. Maybe he just changed his mind."

"Yeah, that sounds about right," Axel said sarcastically. "Kane listening to reason."

"It's been known to happen," Dog said. He stretched his muscles and then checked his Garmin wristwatch. "We're starting to get up there, and we'll be heading off again soon. Better take another sip of water and then pack up." He turned away and walked toward his own pack, apparently planning to do the same.

Axel watched him go, a quizzical expression on his broad face. "You know, I just can't figure these people out. They're at each other's throats practically night and day, but if one of us says something even slightly negative it's like they rush to each other's defense."

"Maybe it is like family," Isabel suggested. "Like siblings who always argue but will beat shit out of any outsider who even looks sideways."

Max hummed softly. "Maybe. Or maybe there's more to it."

~

THEY WERE REALLY CLIMBING NOW. Crampons gripped ground that sloped sharply away, bodies leaned forward, hands and picks became more and more necessary.

As they continued upward, Max became more aware of labored breathing and a pain in his head that was at first scarcely noticeable but steadily grew until it was a pounding that could not be ignored. His movements felt sluggish, even though he didn't seem to be falling behind the others. It was like he was moving in slow motion, and the world had slowed down to accommodate him. Then came the nausea and muddled thoughts, and finally, through a fog, he became dimly aware of something tapping on his shoulder. As if through a tunnel, he heard Axel's voice.

"Max!"

No reply.

"Max!"

He felt strong hands grip both of his shoulders now, bringing him to a halt. The hands, once on the side of his shoulders, now shifted and pressed downward, forcing him to the ground. Max sat down hard, his breathing labored. Thankfully, they had reached a small rock outcrop that provided a relatively level place to collapse.

And then Kane was there.

"Okay," he growled, "looks like we have our first casualty. Symptoms?"

"Huh?"

"Your symptoms, moron. What are they?"

Weakly, Max listed them off.

"Nausea?"

Max nodded.

"Yep. Classic case of AMS."

"AMS?"

"Acute Mountain Sickness. Looks like you're done for this one."

"I don't understand," Max gasped.

"I mean, you're not going any higher this time. Continuing to climb after an onset of altitude sickness of any kind is a really bad idea. I'll give you some oxygen and a little cocktail of pills, you rest for a bit until you're not ready to keel over, and then down to camp you go."

"No, I—"

"I said, down to camp you go. Don't argue with me, Barnes, or I'll rip you apart no matter who your daddy is."

Kane set about gathering the required items, but as he walked away, he shouted at Axel:

"You stay with him, big guy. We can't leave someone alone on the mountain."

"Roger that," Axel called back.

Even sick as he was, Max motioned his two friends close. "He's taking the opportunity to split us up."

"No shit, Sherlock," Axel growled low. "But he's also not wrong. No way are you camping on this mountainside, sick and alone."

"Then Isabel should stay as well."

"I am going on. I feel fine."

"Izzy—"

"Do not call me Izzy. And I will be okay."

"The guy has an interest in you, Isabel."

"What man does not?"

Max gave the lovely woman a disbelieving stare. "Wow! Now that's some confidence." Then his head punished him with a pounding throb, and he hunched his shoulders against the pain.

"Listen, Max, we cannot let the group go on without at least one of us along. If Axel goes, there will be constant tension between him and Kane. I will be able to put them at ease. I will only watch. No trouble." Isabel cast a look in Kane's direction. "Unless absolutely necessary."

Max hated the idea of Isabel going alone with the group, but as with Kane's diagnosis, she was not wrong. He swallowed down the instinctive need to protect her and forced his aching head to nod slowly.

The heavy crunch of footsteps signaled Kane's return, and the conversation ceased.

"Here," the big man said gruffly, shoving a little plastic baggie in Max's face. "A dose of meds for your wittle headache. And here," this time it was a water bottle he handed over. "I'll also leave one of the oxygen tanks in case you need it, but when you go down to base, be sure to take it along so it can be refilled. Any questions?"

Max, who was in the process of swallowing the pills, shook his head.

"Good," Kane said. "We're about ready to head out. If all goes perfectly, we'll be back in camp in three or four days' time. Anything beyond five, and we've run into trouble. Don't come after us—you're not seasoned enough for a rescue. Just call it in."

"Wait ... you destroyed the radio," Axel pointed out. "How are we supposed to call it in?"

Kane grinned. "You think that van was only delivering chang? But don't get any bright ideas. The new outfit is pretty high-tech and requires an access code for anything beyond emergency calls to first responders. I have those programmed in."

"Kind of like a locked cellphone that still allows 911 calls, huh?" Max said, grudgingly admiring.

"Exactly. Perfect setup for when you've got snoopers in the camp."

Kane walked off, waving and shouting at the others to prepare for further climbing.

Axel and Max watched him go, and Max gritted his teeth against the mocking glances and catcalls from the others. Dog had warned there would be razzing, and he had not been kidding.

“So long, Professor Junior!” Grits called out. “Bet you can’t wait to get back to camp to wash out your lace undies!”

“Some woman, huh?” Axel intoned.

“I wish Isabel had slit her throat.”

“Don’t worry; she still might.”

Isabel waved at her two friends as she took up the rear and continued up the mountain. Max watched her go, heart in throat. He admired her strength and calm courage, and it hit him—even though he’d already known it—that he had grown to care for this woman. Yes, he’d wanted her from the moment he saw her, but that had been mere physical attraction. He could no longer pretend his feelings had not progressed beyond the superficial and become something much deeper ... and much more complicated. He was not ready to call them love—and he wasn’t entirely sure what that would entail anyway—but neither was this only a flighty crush.

Axel reached over and tweaked his friend’s ear. “You’re watching her again.”

“I just want to make sure she gets off okay.”

“You know, out of respect for your burgeoning romance, I’m going to pass on the obvious joke.”

“There’s no romance. And don’t be gross.”

Axel chuckled. “Okay, whatever you say. Feeling any better?”

“Yeah.” Max nodded, and was pleased when the motion sent neither a bolt of pain through his head nor a wave of nausea through his stomach.

"Awesome. Let me know when you can toddle, and we'll head back."

"Huh?"

Axel looked at his friend as if the smaller man was a complete idiot. "Back to camp. Per orders."

"Orders?" Max returned an identical expression of his own. "Since when do we follow orders?"

"Um ... never?"

"Exactly."

"Yes, but your health is—" Axel broke off suddenly, his eyes glued to the face of a mountain across the way.

"Ax? Buddy?"

"What?"

"You went somewhere. I'm the one deprived of oxygen, okay? Don't try to steal my moment."

"Sorry, I just happened to look over at the other mountain, and I ... well, I thought I saw something move."

"Oh, good. Because at first, I thought you were having a stroke brought on by the fact you were actually concerned for my health."

"Maybe I am, along with some sort of visual hallucination."

"Must have been pretty big to see it move from all the way over here. Of course, I always forget you have obnoxiously good eyesight."

Axel didn't answer, as he was busy digging in his pack.

"Hallucinations make you hungry?"

"Binoculars."

After a moment, Axel came up with the aforementioned item and held the device to his eyes. He scanned the snow-spotted face of the far mountain for several seconds, before hesitating and then slowly tracking back until finally settling on a single location.

"Is it the eagle I keep hearing?" Max piped up. "Because I've been wanting to—"

Axel shushed him with a wave of one gloved hand. He then tried to adjust the focus of the glasses, but found he couldn't whilst wearing the glove and shook it off with one violent motion. The glove hit the ground and rolled, threatening to pick up speed and disappear down the mountain, but Max reached out and snagged it, his own eyes never leaving the seemingly frozen body of his friend.

"Ohhh, Axelll …" Max sing-songed.

"Sorry," the man said at last. "It's weird. I thought for sure something moved over there, but when I train the binoculars on the spot, all I see is a massive boulder."

"Not so weird. Rocks all over the place up here. 'Up here' basically *is* a giant rock."

"Yeah, but … this rock looks hairy. Is there moss or lichen this high up?"

"Maybe you're not looking straight across. Angles can be weird at this alti—"

"Max."

The odd tone in his friend's voice silenced Max immediately. He waited, not speaking, every nerve in his body tingling. He'd never heard that mix of elements in Axel's voice before: shock, confusion … fear?

"Max," Axel said again. "The rock."

"What about it?" Without intending to, Max had whispered.

"It ... it blinked at me."

"What the—Axel, things can't blink unless they have eyes. Pretty sure rocks don't have eyes."

Axel had dropped the binoculars and looked over at Max. "Dude ... that was the freakiest thing I've ever seen ... or *thought* I saw. I was looking at the, well, the rock and it looked like there were two circular markings. I was focusing on those when—"

"When it blinked."

"Right." Axel brought the binoculars back up and peered through them once more. Then he began scanning the far mountainside almost frantically, whipping the glasses back and forth.

"Ax!" Max shouted. "You're going to break your neck! What are you doing?"

"It's ... it's gone!" Axel sounded absolutely bewildered. "The rock ... it's just gone!"

Getting to his feet, Max grappled for the binoculars, finally wresting them from Axel's shaking hands. He scoped out the mountain thoroughly, but could see no sign of the blinking rock. At last, he dropped the glasses and shook his head.

"Sorry, man. I see nothing."

"But ... but you believe me, right? That I saw something?"

This was also a new tone for Axel: pleading.

"Of course," Max said immediately. "You've always had better eyes than I do, and you're way less prone to dumb things like hallucinations. If you say you saw it, then you saw it."

Axel looked at him suspiciously. "Are you just saying that so I don't think I'm crazy?"

"Nope."

"How do I know?"

"What are you, a woman?" Max burst out. "You want me to prove it? Fine, I'll prove it."

Axel raised an eyebrow, interested. "And just how do you intend to do that?"

"By going over there right now and checking it out."

"You really *are* serious. That's quite a hike."

Max shrugged. "We've got some time. The fastest Kane and Company will return is probably four days. I know he said three, but I doubt that, given all the places they want to check out." He held both hands out from his sides, palms up. "Well? What do you say?"

Axel stared at him for another few moments, and then a giant grin cracked his face.

"I say you're an idiot, and I'm totally in. Let's do this thing."

14

After leaving Max and Axel behind, Isabel resisted the temptation several times to turn around and look behind her. Despite her brave words and insistence that everything would be fine, she did not relish being alone in the group with the rest of the long-time camp members. The only person left with her that she even remotely trusted was Dog, and she resolved to keep just as close an eye on him as she would everyone else. Kane still took up the lead position, followed by Fitch, Grits, Dog, the unknown man, and finally Isabel.

The climbing grew more intense, and she focused on the man in front of her, as a distraction from the increasing exertion. As she watched, she began to realize there was something oddly familiar about him. She couldn't quite put her finger on it, because she had the unnerving inkling she had seen him somewhere before. Not someone she knew well, but more of an incidental, passing acquaintance.

Just past noon, Kane called for another halt and ordered Fitch to set up the camp stove. As he had during the last brief respite, Kane found a place to settle and pulled out his topographic map. Isabel walked over, hoping to get a good look at whatever the big man was studying. As she approached, Kane looked up and gave her a meaningful smile.

"Hello there, beautiful," he rumbled. "How are you finding the climb?"

Isabel shrugged. "It is nothing."

"Well, you must be in even better shape than you look. You sure left your boyfriend in the dust."

"Boyfriend?"

"Professor Junior."

"Oh, we are not romantic," Isabel said hastily, and was then glad the cold weather had already flushed her cheeks.

"Ah, I'm glad to hear that," Kane said. "I somehow got the impression he was pretty annoyed by the fact I was giving you 'the look.'"

"The look?" Isabel felt as if she were asking too many questions, and resented being put on the defensive.

Kane laughed. "Oh, come on, beautiful. You have to know how men see you. And I am no different."

"Max is protective of everyone in his circle," Isabel said breezily. "He would behave the same with Axel, and I can tell you they are not romantic."

"Yeah, but I don't find that big oaf very attractive. Like I do you."

"Mr. Kane, nothing will be happening between us. The

others and I are here only to investigate rumors of the Origin Scroll, as you well know."

"Message received loud and clear, beautiful," Kane said. "But, hey, if you change your mind ... or get lonely during the night ... you know where to find me."

"Yes. At bottom of ravine if you try anything foolish."

Kane laughed again, harder this time. "You keep talking like that, and I may not be able to restrain myself."

"I do not joke, Mr. Kane."

"Fine, fine. I'll keep myself in check, on one condition."

Isabel resented the implication she must bargain for her security, but she was curious. "And what is that?"

"You keep calling me 'Mr. Kane' in that sexy accent of yours." The big man gave her a luxurious wink, and Isabel responded with an equally luxurious roll of the eyes.

Isabel pointed at the map, eager to change the subject. "What is it you are studying?"

"This is a topographic map of the surrounding area," Kane said, thankfully following this new thread of conversation. "Aside from a coded layout of the terrain, it's also marked with key locations discovered by previous expeditions. So we don't double up on stuff and waste our time."

"I think the idea was we would start fresh," Isabel pointed out. "There may be things at some of the sites other explorers did not see."

"So you're telling me you want to start from square one?" Kane's voice suggested both annoyance and disbelief. "That will take us a lot more time than I anticipated. And I told those two we left behind we'd be back no longer than five days. If we start checking all these markers, we're gonna be a lot longer than that, and they'll send out some sort of rescue team."

"Then we will investigate the ones we can, and then head back to camp. New expeditions can be formed to investigate the others."

Kane looked at her, his piggish eyes bright. "Why do I get the feeling you're taking over for me? I don't think I like that. If you were, well, not *you* I'd be forced to remind you who's the boss around here."

"It is my understanding this entire expedition was to be led by Maxwell Barnes. You and the others were to play parts of guide and host."

"Then we may have a misunderstanding about proper roles," Kane growled. "And when we get back to camp, the only way to solve this is probably to place a little call to the university and see what's up."

Inwardly, Isabel cursed herself for pressing the issue, and hoped Max and Axel would find a way to contact the professor again prior to the larger group's return to camp. However, she forced her expression to remain neutral and instead peered at the map.

"What is our first stop?"

"Well, if we were going to focus on the locations that wouldn't, you know, waste our time, our first stop would probably be reached first thing tomorrow morning. But if we're starting from damn square one, then we're just about there."

Kane pointed, and Isabel turned her head to follow the gesture. At first, she saw nothing, but then could just make out a dark object rising beyond an outcropping of rock about a hundred yards away.

"And what is that?"

"Absolutely nothing," Kane answered, "Which is why it's not worth checking out. But if you're going to be precious about this, we'll stop and have a look." He closed the map, folding it up and slipping it into a large pocket on the side of his parka. "But first, we'll have a hot lunch to warm everybody up from the inside." He then began walking over to where Fitch had managed to get the camp stove running. "All right everyone," he said, raising his voice even louder than necessary. "Let's eat, because then we've got a pointless little detour to make and you'll want to be nourished and rested."

A chorus of groans filled the mountain air.

THE TOPOGRAPHY between where Axel and Max had stood and the place where Axel had seen the blinking rock could not rightly be called a valley, even though it was an area of lower elevation between two mountains. It was, more accurately, a saddle that connected the mountain they had been climbing with the group and a second, higher peak. In any case, they still needed to descend a ways and cross the saddle area before making the climb of the new face.

By the time they reached the lowest point of the saddle, Max was feeling mostly recovered. The headache and nausea were gone, and his breathing was almost entirely back to normal.

"I still feel like I have to tell you this," Axel said. "Even though I am 100% on board with the plan."

"Consider it said," Max replied, knowing what his friend was about to say and not wanting to hear it.

"Nope, sorry, that doesn't cut it. As your friend, I am saying you should probably return to camp just to make sure there won't be any further complications from the AMS."

"Thank you, noted, and shut up."

"Okay."

As the two ventured forward, the sun glinted off the snow and cast a golden, brilliant light on the surrounding peaks. The crunch of their boots on the snow-covered ground punctuated the stillness, as if the world had surrendered itself to the grandeur of the moment. The cold air nipped at their faces as they trudged onward, their breaths visible in the icy air, leaving a trail of misty ghosts behind them.

Max felt incredibly alive. He filled his lungs and took in the view: massive boulders and peaks stabbing upward, piercing the otherworldly blue of the sky. The sight was somehow alien and familiar at the same time, like someone returning home after a very long time and seeing even the simplest things through new eyes.

They stopped at regular intervals and used Axel's binoculars to scan the face of the approaching mountain, but were unable to detect anything similar to what Axel had described previously. At one point, Max swung them around and caught a glimpse of the other group.

"Looks like they've stopped," he said. "Probably time for lunch, huh?"

Axel checked his watch. "Actually, it is, but I'm feeling okay, so if you're up to it how about we eat on the move and keep going?"

"Works for me. Frankly, I'm feeling better than I did before we even set out this morning. I think recovering from AMS turns you into a superhero."

"Oh good," Axel said dryly. "Then why don't you just pick me up and fly us over to our destination?"

"I'm not that *kind* of superhero."

"Naturally."

The two paused briefly to retrieve snacks from their backpacks and then munched casually as they moved across the rocky terrain that was now mostly covered with snow. At the lower altitude than the one they had descended from, Max found the conditions just about perfect. The air, while certainly not as oxygen-rich as sea level or even basecamp, was still more than manageable for Max, and he knew exertion at this level would prepare him for later climbs that would likely prove even more challenging. He also knew it would have been a much better idea to spend time doing lesser climbs, acclimating his body to the extreme conditions, but he had—foolishly, he now realized—not wanted to spend the time. Additionally, he had overestimated his own level of fitness. He was fit and he was athletic, but comfortably existing at these elevations was much different than exploring the desert or hacking one's way through the jungle. Both strenuous, both extreme, and both unique.

The audible duet of their feet in the snow gave Max an almost comfortable feeling. He loved having Isabel on their team, of course, but trekking now with only Axel brought back good memories of the times when it had always been the two of them. They had covered a lot of ground together, gone through many dangerous circumstances, and cheated death and serious injury more times than they could have reasonably expected. The addition of Isabel was, without question, a positive development; but sometimes it was nice to revisit the simplicity of the past.

Thinking of Isabel reminded Max of the other group, and he took a glance over his shoulder, even though he knew he would never be able to see them with the naked eye.

"I'm assuming if we saw the group through your binoculars, they could see us," he said.

"If they're looking," Axel replied. "But I don't know why they would. And even if Kane did happen to see us ignoring his orders, there's not much he could do about it right now, unless he sent one of his little toadies to give us a stern lecture."

"I almost hope he does," Max said. "I wouldn't mind teaching Fitch a lesson or two."

"Down the road, you may get a chance," Axel mused.

"What do you mean?"

"Well, I could be completely wrong, but something in the back of my brain is telling me this entire expedition is going to blow up at some point."

"Say more."

"Oh, come on," Axel snorted. "This whole thing is

bizarre. At first, I thought it was a simple matter of them not expecting us, or wires getting crossed at the university or something. I was even willing to chalk up Wei's death to some weird Chinese secret police activity. But then Ruo died —in camp—and I think they were actually targeting you and got him by mistake because he happened to be sleeping in your cot."

A little shiver ran up Max's spine, and it wasn't caused by the chill in the air. This had, of course, occurred to him, but hearing Axel say it now somehow felt even creepier. He finished his energy bar and zipped the wrapper into his pack's garbage pouch. Then he took a drink of water. Finally, he answered.

"Let's just walk, okay?"

15

Needless to say, Isabel was not the group's favorite member after Kane went along with her request—or rather, demand—to check out the closest site. The path to the location was not the most treacherous, but it did require a good deal of concentration and effort on the part of the climbers.

Isabel plodded along, understanding all too well her own limitations in the skill of mountaineering. The last thing she wanted was to force the others to come to her aid, and she determined to not only keep up with the group, but to prove herself.

Isabel's life had been fraught with such determinations, and mostly she overcame such obstacles. Her grandmother, the one who had gifted her the intimidating knife she usually carried, had been kind but not coddling. Not the grandmother who baked cookies and spoiled the grandchild rotten. That was not what Isabel had needed growing up, and her grandmother had known this. Isabel had been given what she needed, not what she wanted, as is the case with all well-rounded offspring.

One could possibly make the argument that her grandmother had been a bit too hard on the girl who then grew into a young woman, and there had been times when Isabel would have been foremost among those making that argument. But now that she was older, and had a broader perspective on life, she understood and loved her grandmother for the dogged determination the old woman had shown.

And this is why, in a seemingly contradictory manner, she had both deeply resented and understood Max's decision to accept Crabtree's assistance. Yes, the eccentric and cutthroat billionaire had taken Isabel's grandmother hostage during the adventure of Ahrum, and normally Isabel would have vowed the man's death. And would have, had she not thought him already dead. The revelation he was still living and, no less, funding the expedition once the university support had been withdrawn, came as a shock. However, because of her tough upbringing, Isabel was a realist. She understood one of those realities was that none of them had the funds to continue their adventures alone. And she was also enough of a realist to understand, more often than not, the sources from which money flowed often had moral shortcomings, which is why it simply did not pay to look too closely.

Nevertheless, she thought, *I may still slit that man's throat with the very knife given to me by the grandmother he imprisoned.*

The other thing that kept her from completely

exploding on Max or quitting the expedition altogether, was the decision that her grandmother would not want Isabel to negatively impact her own life for the older woman's sake. As tough of a guardian as she had been, she had always put Isabel's wellbeing before her own, being sacrificial to the extreme. As Isabel looked back on her own upbringing, she understood there had been many times when her grandmother had gone without so that Isabel did not lack. She still flushed a bit with shame as she thought of times in her earlier years when she had railed against her grandmother for such petty things as curfews, not realizing the older woman had perhaps not even eaten that day in order to provide Isabel with the energy to break said curfew.

Children are so stupid, Isabel shook her head at her own youthful petulance.

Isabel knew the greatest gift she could give her grandmother now was to pursue her own life's goals, which included the expeditions with Max and Axel. Grandmother would not want her to torpedo an opportunity such as the Origin Scroll simply for revenge. Isabel still considered a score to be settled, but it would have to wait until another time.

"Hey, beautiful!"

Isabel looked up and snapped back to the present, not having realized she had been years and several thousand miles away. Glancing around, she discovered she had fallen behind the rest of the group and silently cursed herself for having done the exact thing she had determined not to do just minutes before.

"Keep up with the rest of the group, or you might find

yourself wandering down into a place you can't get out of," Kane said.

"My apologies," Isabel said, hurrying to keep up. "It will not happen again."

On this leg of the trip, she didn't have a chance to repeat the mistake, as they were now approaching the site. It had only been about one hundred yards, but the length of a football field took much longer to traverse in these conditions than it would on flat ground.

"Okay, folks," Kane called out. "We're here to see something we've already seen."

As if his words weren't enough, his annoyed tone demonstrated just how pointless he considered this waypoint to be. Isabel ignored the snide remarks and low, mocking chuckles from the rest of the group, and dropped her pack in preparation for exploring.

Isabel found herself standing on a curious flattened area, a small natural platform nestled amid the jagged peaks and precipitous slopes that surrounded them. At the heart of this miniature plateau stood a tall, weathered wooden pole, its surface covered with carved symbols and designs. The craftsmanship was remarkable, the attention to detail revealing the steady hand of a master carver.

As Isabel examined it more closely, she was struck by its resemblance to the totem poles she had seen in photographs of North American indigenous cultures. The similarities were striking, yet there were notable differences as well.

Unlike the totems she recalled, this mysterious monument displayed an abundance of written inscriptions, the language of which she could not discern. The carvings appeared to be a curious blend of script and pictograms, and as her fingers traced the lines and swirls, she wondered if the secrets it held could unlock a hidden history or a long-forgotten tale.

At the apex of the wooden pole, a frightening visage loomed. It was that of a large, hirsute creature, its fierce eyes seeming to pierce the very souls of those who dared to look upon it. As Isabel stood beneath the watchful gaze of the face, the wind picked up, as though the very elements were whispering ancient secrets to those who would listen. Isabel could not shake the feeling that the answers they sought were somehow linked to this enigmatic totem, and that its presence in this remote place was no mere coincidence.

Kane saw her staring up at the face, and he chuckled. “That’s the Migoi.”

Isabel knew something about the Migoi, of course, having spoken with Ruo, but she feigned ignorance.

“Migoi?”

“You got all the way out here without hearing about the Migoi? I would’ve thought that would’ve come up in your research, given you’re searching for something else that may be nothing more than legend.”

Isabel shrugged noncommittally.

“Well, it seems like you’re due for a little education,” Kane said, somehow managing to make the statement suggestive. “The Migoi exists in quite a few different cultures, and its description and characteristics vary quite a bit. But around here it is assumed to be something similar to the yeti. In fact, according to the couple of people I've spoken to who have seen it, it's even scarier."

"People have seen this Migoi?" Isabel asked.

"Or at least they claim to. I've never seen it myself, mind you, and I highly doubt it's real. In fact, anyone who truly believes in the Migoi might also be interested in a little farmland I have to offer."

"But the carving at the top is supposed to be the Migoi?"

"Yep. Looks kinda nasty, doesn't it?"

Isabel didn't answer but continued toward the wooden pole. She approached it slowly, then—removing one glove —walked around to the rear, using her phone to take pictures of the various inscriptions. She photographed all the way up the pole around all sides and, using the zoom function on the camera, got a close-up of the topmost carving. She began running her hand along the rough wood.

At first, there was nothing unusual about it. The weather-worn wood was coarse to the touch, with a surface that had been etched by years of exposure to wind, snow, and sun. Its once-smooth surface was now textured and bumpy, with deep grooves and ridges that told the story of its long journey through the elements. The wood was a dull gray color, with patches of lighter and darker shades where the sun had bleached it and moisture had stained it.

As she moved in a circle, her hand never leaving the totem, the pads of her fingertips, still sensitive despite the cold, detected a distortion that seemed different from the more random wear patterns caused naturally. She paused, and removed her other glove. Using both hands now, she began meticulously rubbing up and down that portion of the pole. Kane chuckled hoarsely as he watched, but Isabel ignored what she knew he was thinking.

And then, she felt it again ... a small section of wood that was still coarse to the touch, but seemed also uniform in its degradation. Crouching a bit, she looked closely at the area, and then saw that what she had assumed was a wear pattern was actually minuscule carvings that occupied an area approximately a half-inch square. Without even really thinking about it, Isabel reached out with her index finger and pushed inward. At first, nothing happened, so she pressed harder. This time, there was a metallic click and the half-inch square sunk inward.

"What is it?" Kane called out, his voice losing any suggestion of lewdness.

Again, Isabel ignored him, but this time the big man walked over to see what had captured Isabel's attention. When he saw the depressed section of wood, he let out a little whistle.

"Well, now, isn't that interesting." He reached out with his own meaty finger and poked at the button. Again, nothing happened. "It's gotta be here for something," Kane muttered.

Stepping away just a bit, Kane pulled back one massive boot and kicked the totem sharply. The impact sent shivers all the way to the top, and Isabel heard a grinding noise, followed by a series of minute mechanical sounds. Then, a foot-long section popped out about an inch, and then stuck there. Kane moved forward and gripped the protruding section, giving it a good yank. It came away in his hands with a goopy, grinding protest, revealing the interior. Isabel peered inside, her eyes widening at an intricate array of tiny cogwheels. Kane bent over next to her and stared in with his swinish eyes.

"Looks like yak grease," he said.

"Yak?"

Kane pointed into the aperture at the gears. They were coated in some sort of gelatinous substance that had hardened over a long period of time. "Yak grease," he repeated. "They used it to keep things from rotting and rusting. It works like a charm, but eventually it sort of gums up the works. In its prime, this thing would've popped out the moment you pressed it. These days, I guess it took a little extra persuasion."

Isabel looked deeper into the opening and caught a glimpse of something that was neither metallic nor yak. She reached in with two fingers and plucked at it.

"Found something?" Kane asked.

"Yes, I think ..." Isabel lost her grip on the object and had to reset her fingers. This time, she managed to hold onto whatever it was, and slowly withdrew it.

"Looks like a leather scrap," Kane said. "And there's some writing on it. Far too small to be the Origin Scroll, though, if that thing even exists."

Handling it carefully, Isabel held the scrap up to the light. As Kane said, it did appear to be made out of leather and definitely had some sort of writing on it.

"No," Isabel said. "It is not the scroll. Even though we do not know the size of the scroll, this cannot be it. Even though I cannot read the writing, I can tell it is too modern."

"Look at you go," Kane said admiringly. "And I agree

with you. The style of machinery appears to be more of the 19th century variety. Perhaps 18th. Still, it'll be worth taking that scrap down to camp and see if we can get it deciphered. Might be a clue."

"Agreed." Isabel walked back to her pack and, digging inside, retrieved an empty, waterproof packet. Into this, she inserted the leather scrap.

"You don't think I should hold onto that?" Kane said. "After all, I am the climb leader."

"Then you have too much on your mind to worry about a little old scrap," Isabel said reasonably. "I will keep it for now and deliver it to Max as soon as we meet up back at camp."

Kane hesitated, as if he intended to put up an argument, but he apparently decided it was not worth the trouble and nodded. "Fine. Finish up with whatever you still want to do with this site, and we'll head on out. We still have some daylight remaining and no sense in wasting it."

"I am ready now," Isabel replied. "Let us go."

16

By the time Max and Axel had made it across the table and a reasonable distance up the face of the opposing mountain, it was late in the afternoon and they were both feeling mostly spent. The exertion and cold were beginning to take effect.

"I should've bought a deep freeze and hung out in there to train for this," Axel said. "All that time in Central America has made my blood too thin." He looked over at his friend. "Still feeling decent?"

Max dropped off the pack with a deep sigh and pushed himself backward with his hands braced against his lower back.

"I'm not gonna lie, starting to feel a bit rough. Not nearly like I was up on the mountain with Kane and the others, but I could stand a rest." He scanned the area immediately around them. "Would you say we make camp here? You've got one of the tents, right?"

Axel nodded. "It's a small one, though, not really intended for two people. Guess we'll have to get cozy."

"I know you too well to be shy," Max said with a grin.

And it was true; the two had been as close as brothers, and had seen each other at their highest, lowest, and most vulnerable points. Bunking up nice and snug in a tent was not liable to cause any boundary issues.

"Just do me a favor and don't rip the bad ones, okay?" Max said.

Axel shot him an incredulous look. "Are you kidding me? You're the one with those SBDs. Mine might be noisy, but they don't do much damage."

"All bark, no bite?"

"Exactly."

Together, they set about putting up the tent and had it erected in under five minutes. Then Max set up the camp stove and got a fire going, while Axel gathered some snow for water. In a short time, the water was boiling, and Max brewed up some herbal tea for the both of them. When the tea was done, he opened a can of beans and warmed that as well. It was a simple meal, but Max felt like dining royalty as he sat on his pack and enjoyed the beans, steaming tea, and fruit leather for dessert. Axel reached into a side pocket of his backpack and pulled out a bag of jerky. He tossed over a piece, and Max bit into it, groaning with delight.

"You know, I've dined with kings and queens, but this has got to be the most delicious food I've ever had."

Axel started laughing so hard he almost choked on his bite of jerky. "When did you ever dine with royalty?"

Just last week," Mac said, grinning facetiously. "Remember? We ate fast food over that tightly contested chess game."

"You're an idiot." Axel threw Max a piece of jerky, catching him right between the eyes.

Max caught the morsel before it hit the snow and tucked it into a vest pocket on his parka for a midnight snack. "Yeah, but if you actually had higher standards, you would've left me in the dust a long time ago."

"Nah." Axel shook his head. "I don't need that kind of pressure."

After trading a few more good-natured barbs, they set about cleaning their campsite. Then they climbed into the tent and got as comfortable as possible in the close quarters.

"You know," Max said, "this tent actually would be big enough for two people if you weren't the size of both of them."

Axel, who had already turned onto his side away from Max, preparing to fall asleep, grunted. "I can't help but notice you never complain about my massive size when you need someone threatened."

Max chuckled, knowing his friend was right on the money. Max was not a small or weak man, but Axel was in an entirely different league when it came to physical intimidation.

Seconds later, Axel was emitting soft snores, which Max knew would gradually grow in volume throughout the night, until he would be forced to kick his friend in the back to reset the decibel level. It was a routine he had gone through many times throughout their adventures. But this time, as Max struggled to get to sleep—a conundrum that puzzled him given his state of exhaustion—it was not due to Axel's sawing of logs. Instead, his head was filled with questions.

What was his father's actual involvement and what was happening at the basecamp? Professor Anderson Barnes had, in the past, shown a disturbing willingness to withhold information, even if that endangered those he claimed to care about. On the other hand, it was entirely possible the camp was operating on much the same autonomous level as Tibet. Perhaps Kane was simply operating his own mini-kingdom, conveniently far enough away to prevent its true overseer from curtailing his authority.

And what was the real story behind Dog and Dante?

Was Kane really a bad guy?

What about the three Chinese who had met them in Shanghai? And why was Wei killed in Lhasa? Max suspected Ruo was killed by accident, and he himself had been the true target. And as he thought the word "accident," he remembered how Kane had referred to Ruo's death as exactly that.

So many questions, Max thought. *And so few answers.*

Even though the Origin Scroll was certainly his primary objective, and had been from the beginning, Max was also growing increasingly interested in the workings of the base. With any luck, he and Axel could complete their little side quest of the mystery of the blinking rock and still get back to base in plenty of time to tinker around with the radio. Max would love nothing more than to be able to contact his father and get the entire story, even if it meant receiving a serious tongue lashing regarding Max's decision to continue in the absence of either the university's sanction or funding.

And then Max's thoughts were interrupted by a familiar but horrifying sound.

~

THE CLIMBING GROUP made it to the next checkpoint before darkness fell and had enough time to examine the site for Isabel to realize there was nothing to be found. She expected to hear more grumbling, but the others outspoken criticisms had lessened a good deal ever since her discovery at the totem. They were all mostly still annoyed, of course, because this was a naturally salty crew, but they all had to admit that making the early stop had paid dividends. Dog went as far as to openly congratulate Isabel for her ingenuity, and even Fitch gave her a nod of the head as he passed by to relieve himself over the edge of a ravine. Grits and the man she had yet to meet—or even get a look at his face—said nothing, but their silence spoke volumes. If they weren't mocking or criticizing, it was tantamount to tacit approval.

"Okay, people," Kane said, striding into the middle of the group. "It's close enough to nightfall that we should stop here and make camp. We can start fresh in the morning."

The various group members set about performing all the tedious but necessary tasks of prepping a campsite. Soon, their tents were erected, and a small cookstove was steaming. Everyone gathered around in a circle to enjoy the evening meal and recount the events of the day.

As she dined on her bowl of powdered soup and thermos of hot tea, Isabel's mind wandered from the surrounding conversation and traveled down the mountain to wherever Max and Axel might be. She wondered if they had made it back to camp, but there was a little part of her mind that suspected they had taken some manner of detour. She knew them well—Max even more than Axel—and she found it difficult to believe Max would simply follow Kane's orders to the letter without adding at least some sort of additional activity.

As she thought this, she looked out into the darkness that had gathered in the valley below, and then squinted as she caught sight of a tiny dot of light. It was too far a way to tell exactly what it was, but she felt certain it was Max and Axel's campsite.

She smiled softly to herself.

That location was neither where they had left the two men nor in the direction of basecamp. If it was truly Max, then her suspicions had been correct: he had taken a little detour.

She wondered if perhaps they had found something to investigate, but she also knew Max might have included the extra leg of the trip for the sole purpose of not fully following orders. The archaeologist's innate disdain for being told what to do was often one of his less charming traits, but it was also one of the things that made him so good at what he did. On the other hand, Axel was also with him, and while the big man could certainly be just as adventurous as Max, he also tended to be less hotheaded and reckless.

As Isabel finished her meal and was enjoying a simple dessert in the form of a chocolate covered energy bar, night had fully fallen. She tucked away her garbage, cleaned out her soup bowl, and then moved away from the group to relieve herself before climbing into her tent for the night. She took a light with her, but only used it to find her way, choosing to switch it off during in the interest of increased privacy. She had no desire to run the risk of allowing Kane a peek during her most vulnerable.

Just as she was in the process of putting herself back together, her eyes widened at the squeaking crunch of a footstep on snow. She whirled around even as she pulled up the last zipper, and her heart thudded at the sight of the mystery man standing just feet away. He stood there silently —not speaking, just staring. He had been heavily bundled since they left camp and now it was too dark for Isabel to see even as he reached up and pull down the woolen scarf that had covered the lower part of his face. She flicked her light back on and gasped as the beam illuminated the grinning face of Han.

"¡Vaya!"

Han kept grinning. "You seem surprised."

Isabel surreptitiously felt under her coat and gripped the handle of her knife. "Do you not know a woman prefers privacy?"

"I am not here to spy on you, Miss García," Han said.

"Then what do you want?"

"Simple. I am here to kill you."

With that calm and chilling pronouncement, Han raised his arm, and Isabel saw he was holding a pistol. She forced her breathing to remain steady as she looked straight down the barrel's opening—which seemed much larger than it should have been.

"I have questions first," she said.

Han chuckled. "This is not a movie where the villain explains the plot to confused viewers prior to killing the hero. I owe you no explanations. Goodbye, Miss García."

A shot split in the freezing mountain air, and Isabel flinched despite herself.

But the anticipated darkness and oblivion never came.

Instead, Han's grinning face slackened, and his eyes went dead. As he began toppling sideways, his finger squeezed the trigger, causing another sharp crack in the night. But his aim had shifted, and the bullet *whapped* past Isabel's head, so close she felt a whiff of air.

Glancing to her left, she saw a dark form approaching. Too big to be Kane, not tall enough to be Dog. She flashed her light toward it.

"Grits?"

"What, you didn't think I could shoot?"

Isabel did not respond immediately, as she was too busy gathering her thoughts from the insanely close brush with death. Finally, she said,

"I ... I did not think you would care if I lived or died."

Grits huffed out a laugh. "I don't, really. But when you get killed, I wanna be the one to do it. Not some damn man."

Despite herself, Isabel had to smile. Grits was one tough cookie, but something she had learned from her grandmother—one of *many* things—was that everyone had a life story. And that story made them into the person they are at that moment. Grits appeared hard-bitten and calloused, with all the classic femininity sandpapered off—but if there was one thing Isabel could get behind, it was fierce independence; if it was woman against the world, then all the better, because that is what Isabel herself had been forced to do as well. And while Isabel did not possess the bitterness toward men that Grits seemed to, she also knew there were plenty of reasons why that might be the case.

At that moment, Kane's big form burst into view, all bared teeth and flying profanities.

"What now!" he roared, the words more of an exasperated statement than a question.

"That Chinese agent guy was holding a gun to your heartthrob," Grits said bluntly. "It pissed me off."

Kane took a moment to process both Grits' words and the sight of Han's prone, lifeless body.

"Well ... okay, then," he said at length. "Let's haul him back toward camp. Tomorrow, we'll find a nice ravine."

~

MAX DIDN'T BOTHER ATTEMPTING to wake Axel slowly or gently, but went straight to jabbing him hard in the back with an elbow. The big man grunted and tried to scoot away, but the tent was far too small. It took one more jab before Axel rolled over, one eye open, and grunted.

"What the *hell* do you *want*?"

"Did you hear that?"

"No, Max. No, I did not. Because I was, you know, *sleeping.*"

"Wait, quiet!"

"Don't shush me, dude. You—"

And then the sound came again. A guttural growl that started low but quickly grew louder, rising in pitch and volume. It was a dark sound, a threatening sound. The roar of a lion or snarl of a tiger were both terrifying, especially in the wild—and Max had heard both—but this was not a sound that engendered the basic unease of nature's prey, the brutal but natural food chain process. This was underpinned by intentional malice, a desire to do harm for no other purpose than for harm's sake.

Axel's words died on his lips.

"See?" Max whispered. "*That* is why I woke you."

"Was that what I think it was?" Axel rumbled, doing his own impression of a whisper.

"What do you think it was?"

"That sound from the audio file on your laptop."

"That's what it was."

"Shit, man. Just ... holy shit."

"Yeah. I know. I want to turn on a light."

"Don't you dare." Axel's voice was dangerous. "You turn on a light and we're dead."

Max nodded, even though it was too dark for Axel to see. "Ax—do you think that's what you saw, uh, blink at you?"

A few ticks of silence passed.

"Makes more sense than a rock with eyes. And explains why it disappeared."

"How far away do you think that sound was?"

"Hard to say, but it wasn't right outside or anything," Axel said, with shaky confidence. "What about the first time you heard it?"

"What about it?"

Axel sighed. "Was it closer than the first time, when I was asleep."

"Oh. No, it sounded about the same."

"Good, then maybe it's not coming closer. Maybe it doesn't even know we're over here."

A terrible thought hit Max. "I hope it's not going after Isabel and the group!"

"Nah. They're behind us. Whatever made that noise is somewhere ahead."

Max had another thought. "You still have that jerky?"

"A little."

"And I have some in my pocket I saved." Max fished around and pulled it out. "I say we eat all the meat that's left to cut down on attractive smells, you know? Dried stuff in packaging is less worrisome, but this jerky probably wafts for a mile or more, depending on how good a sense of smell this thing has."

"So you think it's an animal?"

Max snorted. "I think it's a fair bet it's not human, right?"

"Maybe it's not either one," Axel ventured, digging in his pack for the rest of the meat.

"Not human, not animal ... what's left?"

Axel did not answer, instead choosing to begin eating the jerky in silence. Awkwardly fumbling in the dark, he passed Max another piece, and the two men consumed what remained, lost in their own thoughts.

An hour later, they had not heard the sound again. All was quiet in the Himalayas, save for the occasional gust of wind, which brought with it the rustling of their tent fabric and the patter of snow as it blew against it.

At last, exhaustion taking hold and gradually overcoming their apprehension, both of them drifted into a light slumber.

17

The sharp tweet of Kane's whistle awakened Isabel. As she lay in her bedroll and gathered her thoughts that had been scattered by sleep, the memory of the previous night crashed into her mind. It was the sort of thing one might dream about and then, awakening, feel relief at discovering it had been only a nightmare. But this was the opposite: waking with no concerns and then remembering the horror a moment later.

"You are María's granddaughter," she told herself. "You will get out of this bed and begin the day."

And so, as with just about everything else Isabel set her mind to accomplish, she did.

The others had already gathered for the morning repast and as Isabel crawled out from her tent, the rich smell of coffee hit her nostrils. She hopped to her feet with more alacrity than had been previously known and strode toward the small cook site, pointing toward the pot as she approached.

"That," she said firmly. "I want that."

Dog chuckled. "It's just the thing to get ya going, that's for sure. Grab your cup, and I'll pour you a slug."

Swearing, Isabel performed an about-face and headed back to her tent to grab the item in question. As she turned, she noticed a still form lying on the ground a few yards away, wrapped in a blue tarp.

Han, she thought, with a little grimace.

She had no real misgivings about the man's death, especially considering he'd made clear his own desire to kill her, but she was uneasy with Kane's fascination with tossing bodies down icy crevasses. That in itself raised all sorts of questions, not to mention she would have liked to ask Han himself a few questions. Finally, although Isabel was appreciate of Grits' intervention, she very much preferred to defend herself, no matter the gender of the rescuer. But Isabel was not going to look a life-saving horse in the mouth, especially since she was in the midst of a group of people she neither knew nor trusted.

There was not much conversation to be had at breakfast, but when the last person was finishing up their coffee, Kane stood up and addressed the group.

"We've got a busy day ahead of us," he said, clasping his hands behind his back in the militaristic attitude Isabel was coming to expect from the man. "I'd like to at least check points on the map before the end of the day, and that's going to require some good travel. Plus, we've got that to deal with." He gave his head a little nod toward the macabre, cigar-shaped bundle a few yards away. "According to my map, there's a convenient little ravine about a quarter mile away. It takes us a little off track, but it should do the trick." He cleared his throat, the sound being the only indication he had given thus far that he recognized the situation as anything but normal. "For now, everyone pack up and get ready to head out."

With that, the morning briefing was over, and everyone dispersed to pack their gear. Isabel knew she could be ready to go in mere minutes, so she took the opportunity to walk over to Kane. Given the man's personal interest in her, she was hesitant to initiate any interactions, but she also wanted answers.

He saw her coming, and his small eyes brightened.

"Do not even think about making any estúpido comment," she said, holding up one hand as she approached.

"Beautiful, I wasn't planning to say anything," Kane said, smiling. "But since you're here, what can I do for you?"

Isabel pointed at Hans' body. "We have one body to send into the ravine, but I thought we would have two."

Kane's eyebrows lifted. "Oh, you're talking about that guy who got killed in Professor Junior's tent."

"Ruo," Isabel said.

Kane nodded. "Right, that guy. Well, it turns out there was another way to get rid of him."

"And that is?"

"You know that van that came into the camp the morning we left?"

Isabel nodded.

"Well, that wasn't just delivering the new radio and supplies for the camp."

"You are saying it picked something up after dropping those other things off."

"Exactly. But now we've got another body, and I'm definitely not hoofing this guy down the mountain to chuck him into the back of the next supply wagon."

"But who is he? The dead man, I mean."

Kane sighed. "You and your friends are really obnoxious, you know that?"

"We make our money by asking questions and finding things out," Isabel said simply. "We are here to find the Origins Scroll, but it seems there are other things at play as well. Things that are resulting in deaths. You do not really expect us to ignore that, do you?"

"I suppose not," Kane admitted, sighing again, heavier this time. "OK, fine. Han, the guy Grits killed last night, has been acting as our liaison with the Chinese government. Kind of an official state babysitter, you might say."

"But he was with the other two men who met us in Shanghai." Isabel was confused. "I thought you said we were not expected? In fact, there were no tents set up for any of them."

Kane shrugged. "I never met the guy who was killed in camp."

"And Wei?"

"I don't know any Wei. Look, Han was kind of a shady character. He came and went from the camp pretty much as he pleased. There were times I wasn't entirely happy with some of the things he was doing, but my silence was rewarded."

"I do not understand."

Kane grunted. "You're like a dog with a bone, you know that?"

"I am just wanting answers."

"Let's just say Han and I had something of a symbiotic relationship. I didn't make a fuss about some of the things he was doing, and he gave us a good deal of leeway concerning the reports he sent in to the Chinese government. If it weren't for him, we probably would've been kicked out of here a long time ago."

"And what kind of things was Han doing?"

Kane shifted uncomfortably. "Well, you might've noticed the basecamp is kinda out in the boondocks. Which makes it unlikely for anyone to witness anyone doing anything someone doesn't want anyone to witness."

Isabel couldn't help but chuckle. "I think that is the most diplomatic thing I have ever heard you say."

"I have my moments," Kane smiled. "Anything else, Nellie Bly?"

"I think that is all for now."

"So happy to have satisfied you," Kane said, giving her a look. "Now go pack up; everyone else is almost ready to rumble."

~

MAX AWOKE NOT FEELING the slightest bit rested. His AMS symptoms had faded, and now he just felt tired. It was a feeling he experienced more times than he could count, given the intense nature of his work and the fact it often took him across many time zones, but its familiarity had not increased its welcome.

Crawling from the tent, he found Axel stirring something in the small cookstove.

"Oatmeal?" Axel offered, holding up the spoon.

"I suppose so, thanks." Max gave a little grimace. "My stomach says no, but my brain says if I don't eat, I'll regret it later."

"Listen to your brain. At least you got some sleep."

"Doesn't feel like it." Max stood up and stretched, then used the knuckles of his fists to knead at the muscles of his lower back.

Axel began divvying up the oatmeal into two bowls. "This should help. It's absurdly good for you, and I tossed in a little protein powder."

"In other words, you ruined it."

"It's chocolate-flavored."

Max winced. "Ax, you know I hate healthy things."

"Oh, I know. And it's going to catch up with you, eventually. In a couple of years or so, your metabolism will come to a screeching halt, you'll pack on the pounds, and your cholesterol will shoot up to dangerous levels practically overnight."

Max chuckled. "You're around the same age as I am."

"It's true, man. Just you wait."

In truth, the oatmeal was not as bad as Max had anticipated, and he knew Axel was right about, well, most things. Not the least of which was how important it would be to have a healthy load of protein in his system for the day's exertions. Max's mother had died when he was quite young, but one of his memories was of her coaxing him to eat morning oatmeal, saying, "Eat your yummy oatmeal, Maxy. It will stick to your ribs."

He shook his head to dispel the painful reminiscence and set about cleaning the bowl.

After they'd packed up, he broached the subject both had been studiously avoiding the entire morning.

"I guess we should actually make a plan for the day, eh?"

Axel nodded solemnly. "Yeah. And I was dreading this."

"Because it was so terrifying?"

"Well, that. But more because I think we're going to disagree on the plan."

Max made a face. "You want to head back to camp, don't you." His tone was flat and almost accusing.

"Hear me out," Axel said, raising one hand. "First, we have no idea what that thing was last night—"

"Which is why we should—"

"I said hear me out."

"Sorry."

"Annnnyway," Axel continued, drawing out the word to highlight his annoyance. "We have no idea what that thing was. Second, it was impossible to tell how far away it was. Third, it's just the two of us, and whatever made that noise sounded a lot bigger than we are."

"You make some good points," Max conceded. "But if we leave now, we may never have another opportunity. I think we should at least go find some tracks. Isn't that what we came over here for?"

"Yes, but that was before I heard that sound. It will take at least a day to look for the location of where the thing was. Assuming we do—what then?"

"Then we'll have some information. Ax, what if that was the Migoi? And really—what else could it be?"

"A bear, perhaps? There are bear in the Himalayas."

Max shook his head. "That was no bear. That wasn't *anything* I've ever heard. Whatever made that sound had to be at least ... what, two or three times the size of the largest bear?"

"Back to my point about there only being two of us," Axel interjected calmly.

They stood for a moment, looking at each other, caught in the impasse.

"How about this," Max said. "We spend today looking for any signs left behind by the non-bear, blinking rock, etc. If we don't find anything, we head back. That should give us another day in camp before Kane and the others get back."

Max had a way of offering a compromise that included what he'd wanted in the first place, but framing it in such way as to make the opposing party appear petty if they refused. Axel clenched his teeth, no doubt recognizing this was exactly what was happening in this case.

"Okay, fine," he said at last. "But if we run across something enormous and hungry, we are not—and I repeat, are *not*—going to engage. Agreed?"

"Of course, not," Max said. "That would be silly. Now, come on—let's get started."

"I see you're feeling newly energized now that you've gotten your way," Axel said, scowling.

Max grinned. "We compromised, remember?"

Axel allowed himself a rueful smile. "This is why I could never succeed in a cutthroat business environment. Fine—let's get this cleaned up. We can leave the camp as it is and plan to sleep here on the way back. No sense breaking the tent down if we're coming back this way."

Max nodded. "You know me; less work is always a good thing." Then he assumed a heroic pose and pointed off toward the forward mountains. "To adventure!"

"And probably a gory death," Axel muttered.

18

THE GROUP TRAVELED FOR A COUPLE OF HOURS BEFORE KANE raised his fist into the air and called for a halt. It had been tough going; the temperature had risen, making the snow heavier and more difficult to slog through. Isabel did not want to reveal how happy she was to take a break, but in truth, she had been struggling. She shrugged out of the straps off her backpack and stood, arms akimbo, taking in deep breaths and studying the terrain around her. Having grown up in Central America and becoming used to the verdant, lush jungle climate, she was still unaccustomed to the cold blue and white palette of her current environment. It was, she had to admit, stunningly beautiful, but was also foreign, and she found it strangely ominous.

"Watch where you step," Kane called out, dropping his own pack and stretching out his muscles. "You can't see it now, but we're on the lip of the ravine. Let's grab Han's body and give him the old heave ho."

Isabel was not yet used to Kane's cavalier attitude concerning death and corpse disposal, and she hoped very much she never would be. If the day ever came when Kane's behavior was not shocking, Isabel feared she had become too calloused even for her own good.

Not everyone shared Isabel's reservations, it appeared, for both Fitch and Grits fell to work hauling the body toward the edge of the ravine.

"Should we say a few words?" Dog asked.

Kane shrugged. "I've never been one for considering the hereafter," he said. "But with Han gone, we're going to have to get another government liaison. If we get the wrong one, that could really cause problems. All that to say, maybe this one is worth a word to the Big Guy."

All the explorers looked at each other, no one wanting to volunteer. Finally, Isabel pointed at Kane.

"As the leader of this climb, I would think you responsible for any ceremonies."

Kane looked at her angrily, but as Isabel had planned, he did not want to dispute her suggestion that he was leader of the climb.

"Fine," he grunted. He looked toward Han's body, tightly swaddled in the tarp, and clasped his hands awkwardly over his chest. "For this body you are about to receive, may it flourish and strengthen, glory and forever, and rise again on the third day." He glanced around at the others, all of whom were attempting to suppress their smirks. "You know what, it's good enough. Over he goes."

Without delay, likely spurred on by a desire to move beyond the entire awkward situation, Fitch and Grits each took an end of the grisly bundle, swung it back and forth a few times, and then—on a signal from Kane—sent it sailing off into the frozen abyss.

Kane whisked his hands together, as if having completed a full day's work, and tramped back to his pack. He heaved it onto his back and then pulled out a whistle and gave it a couple quick tweets.

"Let's go!"

Everyone else groaned.

"Aren't we going to take a rest?" Fitch said. "Maybe get a quick snack?"

"You wanna sip of water, do it," Kane barked. "But we're burning daylight."

AS HE AND Axel moved through the snow, Max found himself sweating profusely inside his parka. At first, he was concerned that he was coming down with another case of AMS, but when he mentioned this to Axel, the big man shook his head.

"No, I'm feeling it too. Temperature must be up."

"Great, I hope any sign of that creature doesn't melt away," Max said.

"I don't think it ever truly melts up here," Axel said. "And even if it did, it won't do it before we are done for the day." There was a hitch in his step as he glanced over at Max. "Because we are headed back today."

"I know," Max said, his tone unnecessarily defensive.

"Just checking," Axel said.

They took a short break thirty minutes later, but both were feeling eager to be on with the day's trek. A sense of impending adventure was coursing through Max's bloodstream, giving him that adrenaline high he loved so much. Apart from some good rounds of beer, he had never been one for external stimulants. Even in high school and college, when peers had experimented with such things, he'd refrained. It was not from a sense of moral superiority; he had just found the idea of artificial uppers to be silly. His drug of choice had been high risk, a surging pulse, a narrow escape—and one needed a clear mind to navigate the spots he and Axel had found themselves in. He was feeling that surging pulse now, and it wasn't only because of the physical exertion. He could sense they were onto something, close to something, he just didn't know exactly what. And the mystery made the anticipation all the better.

Finally, just past noon, Axel held out a beefy forearm to bar Max's path.

"You see something?" Max asked.

Axel nodded silently, then moved his arm to point to a specific spot ahead and just to the right of them. Max squinted in the sunlight, which seemed bright even through his tinted goggles. At first, he saw nothing, but as he focused, he seemed to detect small shadowed places in the snow—depressions or dips. He surged forward, feeling Axel's grip on his shoulder but shrugging it off as he moved. A few steps farther, and he could make out exactly what he was seeing.

"We've got tracks!" he said, letting out an actual whoop. Axel came up behind him, but at a much slower pace. Max bent down to inspect the tracks in the snow, and his eyes widened. "Ax? You seeing this?"

A shadow fell over Max as his friend approached, and he heard a muffled oath.

"I will take that as a yes," Max said. "And I agree entirely. Would you look at the size of that thing? And here I thought you had big feet."

"That's at least twice my size," Axel admitted. "It also looks more human than animal. You still disagree with my thought that we should turn around and head back to camp?"

Max hesitated. He desperately wanted to keep going, to get a glimpse of this ... thing, but even he understood how ill-equipped he and Axel were to face whatever had made this gargantuan footprint. So far, the prudent thing would be to head back to camp, wait until Isabel returned, and then embark on a new expedition better prepared and better armed.

Slowly, he nodded.

"Okay," he said, his voice dripping with disappointment. "Let's head back."

~

ISABEL WONDERED if Kane's desire to get moving was evidence that the big man was not entirely without conscience, but knew he would never admit it. Now they were some distance from the ravine, and approaching the next spot on the topographical map. Isabel had heard more complaints from the others regarding the fact they were being forced to revisit sites they had already examined, but no one could deny that Isabel's insistence on thoroughness had already produced results. She also knew they only had another day or so before they would need to begin planning the return trip, and she wanted very much to find something else before time expired. Of course, finding two additional clues was probably too much to ask, but Isabel had always been one for lofty goals.

"Break!" Kane's voice rent the mountain air, and the group broke rank.

Isabel looked around but could see nothing that appeared as a waypoint or point of interest. She dropped her pack and walked over to Kane.

"And what is this?" she asked.

Kane gave her a half-smile. "You said you wanted to visit every place. Well, this is one of the places."

"But I see nothing."

"Nope. And you're not going to. That's why it's a waste of time, Beautiful." He snorted a laugh and walked away, leaving the dark-haired young woman standing alone.

Isabel frowned to herself. Their immediate surroundings certainly appeared bleak and desolate—and they indisputably were—but there had to be some reason this location appeared on the map. Someone had added it for some reason. She simply had to figure out what the reason was.

She went back to her pack for a quick snack and swallow of water, but moved off alone as the others gathered for a rest period. Her muscles and joints were tired and aching, but she didn't dare waste the time necessary to sit and relax. Kane was clearly eager to move on as quickly as possible—already he was casting impatient glances her way.

Taking careful steps, lest she come upon another hidden ravine, Isabel searched the glistening white landscape for anything that might stand out. At first, nothing did, but as she continued moving, she noticed a spot on the mountainside that seemed to bulge outward.

"It could be only a boulder," she said aloud, mostly as a way to keep her hopes down.

And it could certainly be a boulder, but there was something about the angle and position that seemed purposeful. One of the things she had learned about tracking in the jungle was to train her eyes to notice straight lines or perfect right angles, since these did not typically occur naturally. This form under the snow had that same man-made appearance.

Slowing her pace even more, she approached the location, taking the opportunity to look around her to make certain she was unobserved. She saw no one, and so turned her attention back to her objective.

The closer she came, the more certain she was that whatever was hidden under the snow was not simply a boulder or pile of rocks, but when she started digging, she discovered she had been both right and wrong. The concealed form was indeed rock, but had clearly been sculpted by human hands. The surface was smooth and uniform, and as she uncovered more, she discovered symbols engraved on the rock's face. The engravings seemed similar to those on the scrap of leather discovered earlier, but were different enough to give Isabel pause.

"That is a bit beyond my expertise," she said aloud, continuing to displace the snow from the rock.

The more snow she moved, the more carved symbols she uncovered, but at last she felt certain she had revealed the main portion. Reversing a couple of steps, she pulled out her phone and photographed the rock's face, hoping either Max or Axel would be able to shed light on the symbols.

Now that the snow was mostly removed, Isabel began examining where the rock met the side of the mountain. It did not appear to have arrived there on its own. It was placed too precisely, and there was a slight overhang that would likely have prevented it from toppling down to this exact location. Even if this large boulder had rolled down the mountain side, the overhang would've acted as a ramp of sorts, sending the large piece of rock even farther down the slope. As she ran her hands along the outer edge, her fingers seemed to detect some space on one side. Taking out her knife, she probed deeper, and discovered she was able to insert the blade all the way to the hilt with minimal resistance. Her heart thudded, and she gave up the attempt to restrain her rising excitement. This was not nothing ... this was most definitely something.

Now working almost feverishly, Isabel used the knife to clear out the packed snow from both sides of the rock's edges. Once this task was complete, she stepped back to admire her work, and was struck by a sudden realization: the rock was a door. She rushed forward and began trying everything she could think of to move the rock, but nothing she attempted made any difference. She even tried pushing the rock aside on her own, even though it was clearly too large to be moved by one person, even if that person had been as strong as an ox or an axle.

"I will have to get the rest of the group," Isabel finally admitted, gasping for air, her breath puffing out in clouds of condensation.

She took just a minute to regain her composure and then began heading back toward the rest of the group. Then, she stopped suddenly, her ears perking up; she had heard something. It was definitely human, but at first she couldn't decipher exactly what it was. And when she did, she still didn't understand. It sounded like someone was crying.

Moving as quietly as she could, Isabel crept forward, slowly rounding the side of the mountain. As she did, she caught sight of a lone figure standing a few yards away, face buried in hands.

It was Dog.

Isabel's foot crunched on the snow, and Dog whirled around, his hand going instinctively to his pocket. Isabel held up both hands, and it was then she realized she was still holding her large knife.

"Sorry," she said, waving the knife in what she hoped was a non-threatening manner. "I am not going to hurt you. I was using this for some work."

Dog managed a weak smile through his tears. "Okay," he said. "Would you mind putting it away, then?"

Isabel hesitated. She did not personally view Dog as a

threat, but she had noticed his move toward his pocket and wondered what he had been about to withdraw.

"Do you have a weapon in your pocket?"

At first, Dog seemed to consider denying it, but changed his mind. His tepid smile grew a bit wider while also taking on a self-conscious air. "Yeah, sorry," he said. "It's just a little .25 auto. It's not much, but it makes me feel better. Plus, you can hide this thing anywhere."

"I like it," Isabel said, not entirely lying. True, she preferred calibers with a bit more oomph, but she also was intimately familiar with how important an heirloom weapon could be. "But that does not explain why you are here, and why you are ..."

"Bawling my eyes out?"

Isabel nodded, not wishing to embarrass the man. While it was certainly true that men were capable of shedding tears, most did not want to be reminded of it. But Dog simply shrugged.

"I hate taking this trail," he said.

"And why is that?"

Dog turned and pointed. Isabel followed his indication, and then saw it was a good thing she had moved so carefully when she had first left the group. There, just beyond a low rise in the terrain, was a dark crevasse. She moved forward a few steps before Dog held out a cautioning hand.

"Careful," he said. "It drops off quick, and the lip is deceptively sharp."

Isabel leaned forward to get a better view, and her breath caught in her throat. Dog had not been kidding. A deep, dark crevasse yawned beneath her, its walls encrusted with ice. She could feel the cold emanating from the abyss, and it seemed to chill her entire body beyond what the current ambient temperature would allow. Isabel took in a deep breath, trying to steady herself. The crisp, cold air filled her lungs, and the wind whistled past her ears—a howling symphony of sound.

Instinctively, she backed up, and Dog huffed with grim amusement.

"See what I mean?" he said.

Isabel looked at him curiously. "This is why you were—" This time when she broke off, it was not in deference to the man's feelings; this time, she understood. "This is where it happened," she said.

Dog nodded, and when he spoke, his voice was dull. "Yeah. Right here. In fact, if we were to dig down in this snow, we'd probably find the piton still driven into the rock. Like I said, the lip of this ravine is pretty sharp. It's frayed the rope, and ... well, you know the rest."

"Dog," Isabel began, her voice soft. "Why do the others not believe you?"

Dog shrugged. "I've never been all that popular with the people at the camp. Dante was. I was new. Dante was a long-timer."

"But the others seem convinced of what they saw. Especially Fitch."

"Fitch sees what he wants to see," Dog said sadly. "And once he's made up his mind about something, there is no telling him different. If you try, it only makes him dig in his heels even more."

Isabel stood there, unsure what to say, or even if she should say anything more.

She was saved from deciding by Kane's loud voice.

"Now we're missing two more climbers? Worst expedition ever!"

Isabel chuckled. "I think we should be getting back to the others."

19

KANE STOOD BEFORE THE UNCOVERED BOULDER AND reluctantly nodded his head. "Okay," he said, his voice grudging. "So we missed a few things in the early expeditions. Good eye, Beautiful. Although, this now makes more work for us."

"And how is that?" Isabel asked.

"Well, now we have to figure out what to do with this thing."

"Is that not why we are here? Is that not why the basecamp exists?" Fitch emitted a horse burst of laughter. "I guess that depends on who you ask."

Kane shot him a harsh look, and the other man's mirth dried up. "On the other hand," the big man said, "I don't know that we could move that thing, even if all of us try together."

"But we *can* at least try," Isabel said firmly.

Kane sighed. "Fine, we'll give it a go. But just judging

from the size of that thing, I wouldn't get my hopes up." He motioned to the others, and they all found a place to rest their shoulders in preparation for a concerted heave-ho. "On my signal," he commanded. "One ... two ... three!"

The five remaining climbers all grunted as they put all of their strength into moving the boulder. But even their combined efforts did not result in the slightest bit of movement.

"Hot damn!" Grits said. "It's like we're trying to move the mountain itself."

"But there is an opening," Isabel said, indicating the narrow space she had opened with the blade of her knife.

Kane ran his thick fingers along the edge and nodded. "Yeah, you're right about that. I'm just not sure how we'd move this thing. It's not like we can just drive a Cat up here."

"We have a heavy-duty jack back in basecamp," Fitch said. "Even that would be a pain to have on a climb, but it would be possible. That's assuming it's even that important to move this hunk of rock in the first place."

Isabel looked at him in disbelief. "What are you talking about? Of course, it is important to move it!"

"Look, you're coming at this from the perspective of an adventurer," Fitch said. "We're just basecamp yeomen who keep the place running until someone 'important' shows up." He made a point to create air quotes around the word "important."

"And now this is part of your job," Isabel countered, her voice taking on the stubborn quality her abuela had always despised. "We will come back to this at a time we have the proper equipment."

Kane cut in. "And that time is not now. Let's make our lunch stop here, and then we'll move on a little farther. Tomorrow, we should reach the last spot on this climb before we need to start heading back."

~

MAX HAD SPENT a good deal of the trek back to the tents complaining, to the point where Axel had to threaten to stick him headfirst into the snow to shut him up.

"We're planning to come back," the bigger man rumbled. "So, cool your baby jets."

Max opened his mouth to retort, but then stopped short. "Hey, Ax?"

"What now?"

Max pointed. "Would you mind casting those stellar peepers at our tent site real quick?"

"What am I looking for?"

"Just do it."

Axel did as requested and then swore softly. "That's not good."

"You see them too?"

"If by 'them,' you mean several people occupying our campsite, then yes. What should we do?"

"I'd say we go around them and leave the tents as a sacrifice to the mountain gods, but I think they've seen us."

Indeed, the figures at the tent were now stirring with activity. It was too far a distance to make out much, but it appeared there were several men now standing and looking in their direction.

"I suppose we should face the music," Max said, as they both continued walking. "You wouldn't happen to have Wei's pistol handy, would you?"

"It's in my pack, but maybe we shouldn't go in hot. Besides, I prefer my 1911. Too bad we flew commercial. Next time, if you're going to work with that ass Crabtree, make him spring for charter.

Max grunted. "I think instead of having a girl in every port, we should have a weapon in every city. That way, it's just there when we land."

"I think we'd need higher security clearances to pull off something like that."

"We should look into it."

"Okay," Axel said, rolling his eyes. "I'll schedule lunch with the president and take care of it."

As they approached the campsite, more details became clear. There were three men, all dressed in traditional Tibetan attire with heavy cloaks worn as the first layer. Max noticed the men's boots, which were also of regional construction. Two of the men had red boots, while the third sported an intricately decorated pair. The trio stood in roughly pyramidal order, with Mr. Fancy Boots at the apex.

Max expected the men to begin walking forward to meet them, but instead, they stood as silent statues in the middle of Max and Axel's camp, waiting to be approached.

Nice power move, Max thought.

Don't worry, Paranoia said. *When they kill you, it won't really matter.*

Ugh, you again? I'd thought you'd decided to leave me alone.

I missed you. Didn't you miss me?

Max grimaced. *If by "miss," you mean did I notice you were gone, yes.*

You know, just once it would be nice if you considered my feelings, Paranoia said. *I'm always thinking about yours.*

"Then why don't you just leave me the hell alone?"

Max heard a groan from Axel and realized he'd spoken this final line out loud. He tensed and looked at the man who appeared to be the leader of the trio. Mr. Fancy Boots had raised one eyebrow and now wore a cryptic smile.

At least he doesn't look murderously angry, Max thought.

"Well, that is one way to greet a guest in your camp," the man said.

"Sorry," Max said, flushing. "I was ... er, it wasn't about you, it was ..."

The man waved one hand. "It is nothing. We did come up unannounced and uninvited. That was very rude of us."

"It is nothing," Max parroted. "Uh, welcome, I guess. How can we help you?"

At last, the man stepped forward. He gave a small bow and said, "My name is Tenzin, and I lead a small group of monks who live here in the mountains to pursue knowledge and spiritual enlightenment."

Max nodded. "Pleased to meet you, Tenzin. I'm Max, and this is my partner Axel."

Axel grunted in greeting, but Max could feel his friend's tension.

"We also consider ourselves something akin to guardians of the mountains," Tenzin went on. "We take our responsibility quite seriously, and so often will check in on visitors to ensure they are doing well and do not need any assistance."

"Oh, we're fine," Max assured him hastily. "We don't litter or anything."

Tenzin nodded. "That is good. And how long are you planning to stay in this vicinity?"

Max and Axel exchanged glances, and then Max cleared his throat.

"Say, Tenzin, I hope you don't take this the wrong way, but ... who are you? Do you have some sort of official authority to be out here asking questions, or is this just something you folks do on your own time?"

Tenzin hesitated, but Max wasn't sure if it was from irritation or simply the man gathering his thoughts. When he spoke, he did so carefully.

"This is not something we do merely for fun, if that is your meaning. Our charge is one of great importance."

"Of course," Max said. "I just mean ..."

He trailed off, unable to craft a suitably diplomatic way to ask Tenzin: *What the hell business is it of yours?*

The atmosphere had changed. Whereas before the air was tense with a sense of uncertainty, there had been no outward feelings of animosity. However, Max now felt a shiver of danger drift through the air, making the hairs on the back of his neck stand on end.

Tenzin's eyes darkened. "I really must insist you answer our questions. There is no need for this to become unpleasant—but, as I said, we take our responsibility quite seriously."

The two factions stood looking at one another for a

moment, and Max felt as if he were standing on a dusty Main Street at high noon, waiting for the opposing gunslinger to make the first move.

"Fine. What do you want to know?"

The tension had grown so thick that Max almost jumped at Axel's deep, rumbling question.

Tenzin smiled and nodded. "Very good. Let us start at the beginning. What is your business in these mountains?"

Again, Axel took the lead. "We're here on a research trip for an American university. Gathering data. Climate stuff, you know." He chuckled and waved one large paw to indicate how tedious he found his job.

"I see." Tenzin's darkened eyes narrowed. "And you are associated with the basecamp?"

"Oh, so you know about that?"

"It is well known to us," Tenzin confirmed. "You are newcomers?"

"Yes, we only arrived a few days ago."

"And your mission is only the gather of climate data?"

"That's right."

"And how long are you planning to remain?"

Axel hesitated. "That's unclear. We had some issues with our camp radio, so we haven't been able to speak at length with our university contacts."

"I see," Tenzin repeated solemnly. After a moment's consideration, he gave a decisive nod. "Very well, then. You have a week."

Both Max and Axel stood, struck dumb for a moment. Then Max said,

"I beg your pardon?"

"I believe I spoke clearly," Tenzin said, a steel edge entering his voice. "You have one more week to gather your scientific data, and then you must be gone from these mountains."

"Now wait just a—"

"The matter is settled," Tenzin interrupted, bringing one open hand downward in a chopping motion that Max found unspeakably obnoxious. "We will be checking on your progress. Please do not remain beyond what has been allotted."

"And if we do?" Axel growled.

Tenzin demonstrated a thin smile. "Then these vast mountains shall become an even larger place. Large enough to swallow you up."

20

ALTHOUGH ISABEL WAS BATTING A DAMN GOOD AVERAGE FOR finding interesting things at locations previously deemed barren, she still received a decent amount of verbal abuse after the final waypoint of the climb turned up a big, fat zero. But she didn't blame them. There had been a good amount of excitement—and one death—and everyone was exhausted both physically and emotionally. They were ready to get back to basecamp.

Even Isabel, who considered the outing a mostly rousing success, was looking forward to the admittedly dubious comforts of basecamp. The dining hall with its warm fire not being the least of things she was anticipating.

She was also looking forward to seeing her two friends. Being alone in a group of largely unfriendly faces took an extra toll. Dog was generally pleasant, but even he had dropped into melancholy ever since the experience at the ravine. In fact, he seemed to be avoiding Isabel as much as possible, which she chalked up to the man's embarrassment at having been observed during a private, highly emotional moment.

Now, as they headed back down the mountain, retracing their steps, they found themselves in the vicinity of the mysterious boulder. Isabel could not stop thinking about the giant rock ... and what lay behind it. She was certain it concealed something of importance, and wished she had the training and education necessary to decipher the inscriptions that had been so laboriously carved into the rock.

While she had picked up a good breadth of knowledge while traveling with Max and Axel, this was certainly not equivalent to a formal education in the matters of archaeology. Her background was more complicated than that. After being raised in Central America by her tough but loving abuela, a headstrong, teenaged Isabel had met a man named Francisco Estrada de León, who had swept her off her inexperienced feet through an intoxicating mixture of good looks, charm, and worldly persuasion. He had taken her to his homeland of Spain and shown her many of the finer things of life. Sadly, Estrada turned out to be a very unpleasant individual, and efforts to defeat his evil plans were what brought her into contact with Max and Axel in the first place.

Her time with Estrada had not been entirely wasted, however. An already toughened Isabel had learned how to handle herself around the most dangerous men and even, when necessary, how to kill. But these were—for Isabel—all practical skills, and not useful when attempting to decode ancient symbols.

Kane's whistle warbled through the cold air, calling a halt.

"We'll rest here," he barked. "Just a few minutes, then we're off again. I'm ready to get the hell back home."

As she sat down on her pack to catch her breath and have a power snack, Isabel thought it interesting he'd referred to basecamp as "home," and wondered how long he and the others had been here. They certainly seemed comfortable there, and she had heard nothing about anyone leaving or any pending staffing changes. To Isabel, it almost seemed as if the only way to leave basecamp was to die.

The thought chilled her more than the temperature, and she was considering asking Dog about staffing concerns when she heard a familiar voice, one that sent a thrill through her entire body.

"Hello in the camp! Anyone home?"

"Max?"

Isabel jumped up from her pack, barely registering Kane's smirk at her enthusiastic reaction. She ignored him, even though she was a bit disappointed in herself for how she had instinctively responded.

And there they were, Max and Axel, trudging into the group's midst like a couple of long lost hobo brethren.

"What the hell?" This shout from Kane, who came barreling through the group like a freight train. "I thought I told you to get your ass back to base!" The man had his hamhock-sized fists clenched, and Axel stepped forward to intercept.

Max stood his ground. "We were, but we ran into some interesting folks along the way," he said, omitting the fact this had happened during the duo's little detour.

"Folks?" Kane squinted. "Who?"

"They didn't say. But they left us with the distinct impression that they wanted us to leave."

"What impression?"

"They told us to leave. They gave Axel and me a week."

Kane relaxed his body and crossed his arms. "What did these 'folks' look like?"

"There were three of them, but one seemed to be the leader. All dressed in traditional Tibetan garb, with slightly creepy cloaks. Oh, and they had interesting boots."

"How so?"

"Well, they just seemed custom made in the traditional style. Certainly not something that would come off a mass production assembly line. The leader guy wore fancy embroidered ones, and the other two had red."

Something like recognition flickered in Kane's narrowed eyes.

"That means something to you," Max stated.

Kane coughed. "What did you tell them?"

"That we were scientists gathering climate data for an American university."

"And they bought it?"

Max shrugged. "Well, they didn't kill us. But they also gave us only a week to finish up and leave. So, I'm not entirely certain."

Kane was silent for a few seconds, then emitted a low growl of annoyance that end on a crescendo. "Okay, fine! I suppose I owe you idiots some answers. And it's time for a break anyway, so let's have a sit, and I'll tell you what I know."

~

THE THREE ADVENTURERS, plus Kane, sat together with cups of hot tea, while the other three—Dog, Grits, and Fitch—loitered around trying to look busy. Although having promised to fill them in on whatever secrets he may have been hiding, Kane appeared to be in no hurry. He sipped his herbal teas, snacked on a granola bar, and casually took in the scenery, all the while humming softly to himself.

Finally, Max could take it no longer and burst out, "Well?!"

"Huh? Oh, sorry." Kane did not look sorry and clearly knew exactly what he'd been doing. "I guess I've kept you waiting." He smirked, and Max was tempted to tell Axel to wipe it off.

"You have," he said, trying to remain calm. "You have indeed."

Kane finished his snack and drained the tea. "Okay, fine. I've had my fun. Those men you met were probably Migoi."

"I thought you said the Migoi was creature of legend," Isabel said, casting Max and Axel a meaningful look.

All three knew of the difference between the creature and its followers, thanks to Ruo filling them in during the drive to basecamp, but there may be something to be gained by letting Kane tell things his own way.

"Well, it is," Kane said. "And it's a complete myth. But what is *not* myth is a group of crazies who consider themselves followers of this thing. Guardians, or whatever."

Max nodded. "The leader—he called himself Tenzin—mentioned something about their 'charge' and how important it was. You think he meant the Migoi?"

"Could be," Kane answered. "Or the mountains themselves. Or both. Either way, they're creepy people and have kept an eye on basecamp for about as long as we've been out here."

"Is that why you have the armed guards?" Isabel asked.

Kane nodded. "Yeah. Early on, we had some issues with these wackos sneaking into the camp and stealing supplies. At one point, they even put sand in the generator. That took us down for awhile. Once we started shooting warning shots, they backed off, and we've had something of an informal truce ever since."

"Informal?" Max asked.

"Meaning I've never actually talked with any of them. I'm surprised they approached you directly. Usually, their methods are more ... well, covert."

"Like what?"

"Messages, notes, weird symbolic things."

Max's mind flew back to Lhasa, and the horrific scene of Wei's severed head. And the rolled up note—like a scroll—that had been placed in the head's gaping mouth. He glanced at the others to see if they were making the same connection, but both Axel and Isabel were staring at Kane impassively.

A wild thought suddenly occurred to him. It was something he knew he should first discuss with his partners, but he also felt the time was right. Kane seemed open and, oddly, much less sinister than he had seemed at basecamp.

"Something odd happened to us in Shanghai," Max ventured, keeping an eye on his friends for any subtle "shut up" signals, but seeing none. "We found a bug in a lamp."

"Yeah, that happens," Kane said. "Sometimes the housekeeping doesn't always—"

"No, like an electronic listening device. You think that was the Migoi?"

Kane shook his head. "I doubt it. That doesn't sound like them. Too techy. Plus, they seem to stick closer to home." Then he shrugged. "Of course, I don't really know. Could have been, I guess, but much more likely the Chinese secret police were just keeping tabs on you."

"That makes sense," Axel offered. "They woke us up in the wee hours and we basically fled the city under cover of darkness."

Kane frowned. "That's not something I like to hear. Surveillance by the Chinese is to be expected, but if you sneaked out of Shanghai—well, that suggests you were running from something. I'd ask Han about that, but he's not ... available."

"He tried to kill me," Isabel said.

Max's heart thudded, even though he knew Isabel was fine, as she was sitting directly beside him. "What happened?"

"Grits took him out," Kane said. "And then we chucked his body into a ravine."

"I didn't even know Han was on the climb, but now that you mention it, I guess you are short a person. I thought that was just another guy from basecamp I hadn't met yet."

Max drew in a long breath, and then proceeded to fill Kane in on some of the other events, including Wei's death. The hulking man listened carefully and an unfamiliar line of worry etched his forehead.

"I don't like this," he said, once Max finally stopped speaking. "There's something going on."

"You think?" Axel grunted sarcastically.

Max expected Kane to bristle at the tone but instead he just sat there, musing and rubbing his stubbly chin. At last, he shrugged.

"Well, you've filled us in, so now we have some things to tell you." He looked at Isabel. "You want to do the honors, Beautiful?"

Max felt a flash of resentment at the moniker, but forced himself to remain calm so as not to ruin the moment. They were making some real progress, and he was determined not to torpedo everything with his own jealousy.

Isabel frowned a bit—which Max hoped was in response to Kane's remark—but when she spoke, she kept to the topic at hand.

"Sí. There was, of course, the killing of Han, but we have also found two things of interest to the expedition."

Max's ears perked up. "Do tell!"

"The first," Isabel said, rummaging in her pack, "is this piece of leather. It contains writing I could not read, and is too small to be the scroll, but perhaps contains some clue." She withdrew the specimen in its waterproof packet and handed it to Max, who examined it carefully.

"Where did you find this?" he asked.

"In a wooden monument farther down the mountain. There was a secret compartment in the side."

"Wow," Max said, aware of the inadequacy of the word but feeling truly speechless. As he continued turning the leather scrap over in his hands, Axel picked up the torch.

"What's the second thing?"

"A giant boulder."

This snapped Max out of his revery. "Iz, we're on the side of a mountain."

"But this one—" Isabel cut off with a little growl of annoyance. "Oh, you will just have to see it."

Max noticed she didn't confront him about the shortening of her name and experienced a minor thrill over the fact.

"Wait," he said, "so it's close?"

Isabel pointed. "It is that way."

21

MAX STOOD BEFORE THE BOULDER AND USED HIS GLOVED hand to whisk away a light dusting of snow. He could see where Isabel had used her knife to uncover a sliver of space between the side of the rock and the mountain itself, but it was too narrow to see through. He looked at the engravings and searched his brain for some recognizable connection. Although he had spent some effort boning up on Tibet in general prior to the trip, there had certainly not been enough time to delve deeply into the language or dialects—an endeavor that would take a lifetime. However, he did find a couple of items that seemed familiar, and was fairly certain he'd seen them on both the leather scrap and the digital images of the heavily damaged scroll on his laptop. Knowing what these symbols meant, however, was another thing altogether and far outside of his expertise.

"We should get some photos of this thing," he said, feeling in his pocket for his phone.

Isabel grinned. "I have two walks ahead of you."

"Steps, you mean. You're two *steps* ahead of me."

"As I usually am."

Max chuckled and shook his head. "You're a confident one." *And I like it*, he wanted to say, but refrained given that Kane was standing right behind them. "Any way to get this thing open?"

"We all gave a try," Kane said, stepping forward. "But it's solid. I don't even think Hulk and I could budge it."

Max took another look at the rock and nodded. It was huge and seemed to sink into the ground with its own weight. He glanced up and tried to see the top of the rock, but it was a few inches too tall.

"Hey, Ax, gimme a boost."

Without asking why, his friend bent over and interlocked his fingers, creating a step. Max put one foot into the hand-step, then leaned against the rock while Axel stood up, providing the needed few inches.

"This is strange," Max said, running his fingers along the top.

Isabel looked up at him. "What is it?"

Instead of answering, Max held out one hand. "Can I borrow your knife?"

"Oh, Max," Isabel sighed. "When you borrowed my knife in Guatemala, I said you should feel privileged, because I never let anyone else use my knife. I did not know it was going to become habit."

"Hey, this is different," Max smiled. "This isn't *the* knife. I also recall you saying it would cost me later—more than I could afford."

"That is coming," Isabel said vaguely. She withdrew the knife and handed it up to Max, saying as she did so, "And now it will cost you twice as much."

"Oh brother," Axel groaned.

Kane let out a lascivious chortle.

Max gave them both a dirty look. "Why are you both assuming we're talking about sex? We're not even together, okay?" Feeling annoyed, he grabbed for the knife, almost slicing a finger through his carelessness. Once he had the weapon firmly in hand, he began using it to remove the packed ice and snow from along the top of the boulder, much as Isabel had done along the sides.

"I sort of assumed this was just leaning up against the mountainside," Max said. "But what doesn't make sense is that there doesn't appear to be anything holding it up." He pushed himself away from the rock and jumped out of Axel's hand-step, landing on the ground with a crunch of snow and rock.

Kane frowned. "What are you talking about?"

"It's open at the top, and it's open on both sides. I thought maybe it was a door of sorts, but there's no way for it to swing open or to the side. Nothing seems to be connected. It's just sort of standing there."

"Must be sunken, then," Axel said, kneeling to examine the base.

The boulder did appear to be embedded into the ground, which one would assume if it fell down the mountain, but as Isabel had surmised earlier, it didn't seem likely it would stop at this precise location. In addition, this was not the softer earth of the valley; this was hard mountain rock.

"Help me move some of this snow," Max said, dropping to his knees.

Together, they made quick work of the snow around the base of the boulder, and Max—still in possession of the knife—used the point to clear the remaining frost.

"Whoa, people," Max said, peering downward. "It looks like this thing is set into a purposely constructed groove. Am I nuts?"

"Probably," Axel said, "but that doesn't mean you're wrong. Looks that way to me, as well."

Max groaned in frustration and leaned against the boulder, bracing himself with one hand. As he did, there was a slight grinding sound, and the rock under his hand depressed about an inch. He jumped back, and when he released his hand, the portion of rock popped back into place.

"Okay, I'm definitely not nuts. Did you all see that?"

The others were looking on with gaping mouths and staring eyes.

"Oh, we saw that," Kane grunted. "What the hell was that?"

"I would think it was a hidden key, but it doesn't appear to have moved the door at all."

"Try it again," Axel prompted eagerly. "Actually, no—I want to."

He stepped forward and pressed where Max had a moment before. Again, a small section of rock sunk inward, but nothing else happened. When Axel released the pressure, the rock slid forward, leaving no trace.

"I think the touch point is the symbol," Max said. "But I don't know why it doesn't work."

"Could be it is old," Isabel suggested. "At the totem where I found the scrap, the inner workings of the lock were stuck."

"Until I fixed it with my boot," Kane interjected.

Max considered this. "Maybe," he said. "But that grinding sounded like stone on stone, not metal machinery that can rust or freeze up with disuse. Kind of like the engineering in Aztec or Incan temples. It lasts forever."

"It's a lot warmer where one finds Aztec or Incan temples," Axel pointed out.

Max nodded. "True. Still ..."

He took a step and now looked at the engraved symbols with new eyes. Instead of trying to decipher them individually, he took them in as a whole and, when he did, a sort of order emerged. It reminded him of the 1990s fad where one would press their nose against the print and then slowly back away until the three-dimensional image popped into view. In this case, though, it was not a dimension but rather an organization that became evident.

"Look at these symbols," he said, pointing at a couple of them. "They don't appear to be placed randomly. It's like a grid system."

Reaching out, he pressed on a random symbol and that section of rock sank inward with the same grinding sound as before. And, again, when he released the pressure, it slid back into its original position. He turned to Isabel.

"Mind if I take another look at that piece of leather?"

She produced it, and Max frowned at it in concentration, then looking back at the boulder.

"Unless I'm sadly mistaken, every single symbol on this scrap has a matching symbol on the rock's face." He looked at Axel. "You don't suppose—"

Axel interrupted. "That if you press the symbols in the same order as they are printed on the leather—"

"That it will open the rock!" Isabel finished.

"What is this, some terrible vaudeville routine?" Kane growled. "It sounds crazy, but what do we have to lose. Get on with it."

Holding the leather in one hand, Max used the other to carefully press each symbol in order. Each time, the rock sank inward and then slid back. As he pushed on the last one, Max held his breath, preparing himself for any possible result.

He needn't have bothered.

Nothing happened.

A loud guffaw issued from the rear of the group as Fitch sent up a derisive hoot. The three explorers looked at each other, and Max cringed. Failure was commonplace in his field; in fact, the rarity of true successes made them all the sweeter when they finally came. But it was galling to fail in plain sight of people who both expected and possibly hoped for such failure.

"Well, that was anticlimactic," he muttered. "And it made so much sense."

"Maybe too much sense," Axel replied. "Try some other variations."

"Like backward?"

"Exactly. If that doesn't work, then perhaps alternate the symbols."

"Alternate?"

"Yeah, like do every other symbol, then go back and do the ones you skipped."

"Aw shit," Kane groaned. "We're going to be here awhile, aren't we?"

He did not receive an answer.

Apparently taking that as an affirmative, he turned away and gestured to the others.

"Come on, folks. We might as well set up for the night. By the time Holmes and Watson get done fiddling around, it'll be too late to reach the next safe camping site. But make no mistake—we're leaving bright and early. The next person who causes a delay gets chucked down with Han."

22

MAX LAY IN HIS TENT, BLOCKING OUT AXEL'S SNORING, HIS mind racing over the problem of the boulder. He was absolutely convinced that, one, it barred the entrance to a cave and, two, there was a way to move it and, three, the symbols were the key. There was simply no chance such an intricate and complicated mechanism had been devised for no purpose. They just had to figure out the correct pattern or order.

He clenched his fist and felt like throwing a toddler's tantrum. It was all so frustrating. He, Axel, and Isabel had spent another hour at the boulder, trying every type of iteration and combination they could think of, even to the point where Axel began writing them down so they wouldn't forget and start repeating. Max's hands grew tired, and they then took turns pushing on the sections of rock.

But to no avail.

Max got so used to hearing the grinding stone that he

could hear it even now as he lay in his tent and felt sure he would hear it for many nights to come. It was seared into his brain, and he had come to associate it with the definition of failure.

Max was exhausted, frustrated, embarrassed, and run down. The climb had taken a good deal out of him, and he desperately wanted a win. And after returning to basecamp, he would be immediately presented with the problem of contacting his father. That, however, might not be as big of an issue as he'd expected. Kane's overall attitude had thawed a good deal, and Max was beginning to think he might be turning over a new leaf ... unless the big gorilla had another reason for the sudden change.

I wonder if it's Isabel, Max thought, cringing. *If that's so, he's liable to be worse than ever once she manages to convince him there's no chance ... there's no chance, right?*

Max groaned aloud. His mind was starting to go off the rails, and he knew it was only a matter of time before Paranoia showed up to get in on the action.

To his surprise, however, it didn't make an appearance, and Max eventually drifted off into a fitful sleep.

"Max!"

The hissing whisper stabbed the explorer in the ear like an aural poker, and he came up sharply, his eyes wide and frantic.

"Huh? What?"

"Shhh!"

A hand clamped over his mouth. He started it struggle, but then came out of his sleep stupor enough to realize it had been Isabel's voice.

"Isabel?" he asked, even though with her hand over his mouth, it sounded more like, "Eshubeerr?"

"It is me," she said, still whispering. "If I take hand off mouth, you will stay quiet?"

He nodded, and she slowly relaxed her grip.

"What are you doing here?" Max asked, keeping his voice low.

"I thought of something. About the symbols."

Max curled his lip. "I think I've had about all I want of those for the day. My hand are still sore from pressing on that rock."

"You are a baby. But listen! I took some photos of the totem where I found the leather, and I was looking back over them just now."

Isabel pulled out her phone and turned it on, illuminating both of their faces in its blueish glow. A little surge of excitement kindled in Max's stomach, but he forced it to remain nascent.

"Did you find anything?" he asked, keeping his voice purposely skeptical.

Isabel nodded. "I think maybe." She tapped the screen and then swiped a few times. "Here," she said, turning the screen so Max could see what she was indicating.

Almost at once, he saw the exact symbols that were on both the rock and piece of leather.

"I see the symbols," he said. "But Iz, we tried just about every possible combination."

Impatiently, she tapped the side of the phone with her index finger. "But look closer at the photo. What do you see beneath each symbol?"

Max squinted and then rubbed his eyes to rid them of any sleep remnants. Then he gave up and used his thumb and forefinger to zoom in on the photo. Sure enough, underneath each symbol was a carved arrow, pointed to the right.

"Well, that's interesting," Max said. "And the arrows all appear to be different lengths."

There was a slight tremor in the tent as Axel awakened and rolled over.

"What are you two babbling about?" he asked sleepily, giving a mighty yawn.

Neither Max nor Isabel bothered to ask him to whisper—he already was. However, Axel's version of a whisper would be largely unrecognizable as such by most people.

Max quickly brought him up to speed, and Axel took a quick peek at the phone screen.

"What's the significance of the arrows pointing right?" he asked.

"That I do not know. Maybe none," Isabel said. "I think there is more significance in the length of the arrows."

"You don't think that's just an artist's error?" Axel wondered.

Isabel shook her head. "If you look at the rest of the carvings—and certainly the stone itself—there is nothing to suggest whoever made all of this was careless. It is all very detailed and intricate."

"I'd have to agree with that," Max said. "I don't think any

of what we're seeing was done without a purpose in mind and carried out with amazing craftsmanship." He looked across the glowing screen at Isabel, who looked gorgeous even at such an hour, in those conditions, and in that harsh lighting. "What are you thinking?"

Isabel grinned. "I think maybe it indicates the—" she motioned with her hands, trying to come up with the proper word "—deepness."

"Deepness? Like, depth? What do you—" Max stopped as he realized what she was saying. "You mean how far we depress each symbol?"

"Sí!"

Max and Axel exchanged a look.

"What do you think?" Max asked.

Axel shrugged. "It's worth a try, I suppose." He started to wriggle from his sleeping bag.

"Wait, we're going now?" Max said. "Shouldn't we wait until morning?"

Isabel scoffed. "Are you forgetting what Kane said about more delay? Do you want to be chuckled down with Han?"

"Chucked. And, no, I don't." Max sighed. "All right, let's do it. We can take our headlamps with us."

The trio bundled up, affixed their lamps, and moved from the tent as quietly as possible. The night sky was just bright enough to allow them to move through the camp without turning on their lights, as they crept along toward the narrow mountain path that led to the mysterious, carved boulder. Max heard the light sounds of snoring from the other tents, and for every pause and hitch, the explorers remained motionless until the rhythm of life resumed.

As they left the camp's boundaries, Max's heart pounded with anticipation. At first, he had been less than impressed with Isabel's hypothesis concerning the symbols, but as he thought about it now, with the frigid night air prickling his skin and frosting his eyebrows, it seemed infinitely more plausible. What else could the arrows mean? There did not seem to be a way to move the sections horizontally, so to Max's mind, not much else remained. Additionally, in his own experience with ancient cultures, little was done without some purpose in mind. Ancients, by and large, had not possessed the luxury of pointless activity, and were also a good deal cleverer than the average modern human might assume. Of course, that assumed this *was* the work of ancient people. The engravings certainly appeared that way, but there was nothing else to suggest such a thing.

"Max, we're here," Axel said, jerking the archaeologist back to reality.

His eyes focused, and he saw the boulder before them. His hands started aching as he remembered the dozens of combinations they had tried on the markings. He looked at Isabel.

"You have that picture on your phone?"

She nodded and unlocked the device's screen. Max looked over her shoulder.

"So I guess we just try them in this order. In the picture, the one at the top has the shortest arrow, so maybe try pressing that one in very, very slowly and see what happens."

Axel stepped forward and located the indicated symbol. Placing his big hand flat on the surface, he began pressing inward. As before, a border appeared around the symbol as that section of rock recessed. This time, instead of pushing it all the way in, Axel eased it back with almost maddening slowness. He hadn't gone far, however, when there was a sudden *click*. Axel pulled his hand back, and they all uttered muffled cries of glee as the depressed symbol stayed put.

"Now the next one!" Max said, practically jigging with excitement.

Axel checked the symbol, then began slowly pressing on it. But no sooner had he done so, than the first emitted the same *click* as before and popped back into place.

"Dammit!" A wave of frustration welled up inside of Max. After the first success, he had been certain this was the answer. "Are you sure you did the right one?"

"I'm sure, okay?" Axel growled out. "And don't even think about blaming me; I'm just as annoyed as you are."

Isabel waved her hand at them. "You will both be quiet."

"Look, we're just—" Max started, but she waved her hand again.

"Shh!"

And then Max heard it too.

A guttural growl that started low and then began gradually rising.

It sounded close—much closer than the other time Max had heard it.

"Did you hear that?" he asked, even though he knew full well they had.

"Uh, yeah, we heard it," Axel said. "And I'd say we should get back to camp, but it sounded to me like it came from that direction."

No sooner had the noise ended than it began once more.

"Aaaand now it's even closer," Axel said. "People, it's coming this way."

Max looked around frantically. His friend was right—the sound was coming from the direction of camp, so that direction was off-limits. In front of them was the boulder, behind was a precipitous drop-off, and the mountain soared steeply upward in the other direction.

"I don't want to say we're trapped, but ... I think we're trapped."

The growling came again.

"Definitely coming this way," Axel said. "Any ideas?"

Max put his head in his hands, willing his brain to think—think—think. There had to be some way—

"The symbols," he said abruptly.

"Look, we tried that already," Axel said. "It was a no-go. Sorry, Isabel," he said, looking toward her, "it was a great idea, but—"

"No, we did it wrong," Max insisted. He was not at all as certain as he sounded, but when one is facing a terrifying, unknown creature, one clings tightly to the first available possibility. "Iz, do you have that leather scrap?"

She nodded wordlessly and fumbled in her pocket, coming out with the waterproof packet. Max held it before his headlamp and then tapped at it with a gloved finger.

"The two things have to be used together," he said.

Axel grunted. "Max, *what* two things?"

"The markings on the totem and the leather. The totem shows the depths of the sections and the leather shows the *order* they have to be pressed."

"You'd better be right about this," Axel said, and then leaped toward the boulder, even as the growling sounded again, this time seeming almost on top of them.

At that moment, Max heard something else—a piercing scream from the direction of the camp.

"Axeeeel—"

"I'm hurrying! Show me those symbols, quick!"

Isabel and Max flanked Axel and held out their respective clues. The big man's head swiveled back and forth as he checked first the order and then depth. He began pushing them inward, one at a time. At first, he went too quickly, and the block reset themselves, causing a duet of groans from the other two.

"Quiet!" he ordered, and then started over.

This time, one by one, the symbols *clicked* into place.

The growling had continued—as had the screaming—and Max found that his hand holding the piece of leather was trembling.

"Hold that still!" Axel demanded.

"Sorry, I—" Max glanced down the path toward the camp. "Oh shit. Oh shit shit shit!"

"What!"

But Max was now rendered momentarily speechless. He stood transfixed, mouth agape, as an enormous, hulking figure rose upward in the darkness, cutting off any possible path of retreat. While its features were mostly indistinguishable, the silhouette was unmistakable, a behemoth of some otherworldly origin. It loomed against the night sky, seeming to block out the moon and stars. The form seemed impossibly tall, with two glowing blue orbs about where

Max would expect the eyes to be. As he watched, they flickered out and then returned.

Almost as if the creature had blinked.

"Axel, you will whack whack," Isabel said, her voice modulated but still shaky.

"I think you mean 'chop chop,'" Max said, his own voice mirroring hers in an odd parody of poise.

Click.

"Got it!" Axel bellowed.

Even as the final section clicked into place, the boulder trembled and then dropped straight into the ground with a loud *kuh-thwunk!*

"Hot damn, it's open!" Max practically screeched, pointing at what indeed appeared to be the newly revealed mouth of a cave.

He pushed Isabel forward, but she needed little encouragement. Together, they tumbled inside the opening, with Axel a close runner-up.

The creature outside let out a deafening bellow and surged forward.

"Lights, I need lights!" Axel yelled, all while using his own headlamp to search the wall around the now-open doorway. "If there's a way to open it, there must be a way to close it!"

The other two turned their own lights his way, fully illuminated the front of the cave.

"There!" Isabel shouted, pointing.

Then Max saw it too—an obviously carved section of stone protruding from the wall to the right of the opening. Axel must have seen it at the same time, for instead of pressing with his hand, he fully committed by throwing his entire body against it.

He and the creature moved at the same time, Axel against the wall and the beast toward the cave's entrance. The moment Axel made contact, the protruding stone sank inward and the large boulder shot upward as if on a massive spring, blocking off the opening with a grinding, crunching, rumbling thud. Pieces of rock and little streams of detritus poured down from the cave's ceiling, and the entire mountain seemed to tremble as the creature outside crashed into the rock barrier. All three explorers covered their heads instinctively, and Max thought at first that whatever was out there might actually be able to force its way through.

But the boulder held.

23

MAX COUGHED AS DUST SWIRLED IN THE AIR, SIFTING through the light of his lamp like grit-laden fairy dust. His heart pounded in his chest, the adrenaline coursing through his veins as a mix of fear and determination gripped him. He turned his head around, back and forth, frantically trying to both gather his own wits and also get a read on their surroundings. The air was heavy with a sense of impending doom, and the deafening roars of the creature echoed through the cavern.

The creature outside now seemed to be throwing its massive form against the rock, and as the beam of Max's light illuminated the upwardly curving walls of a cave, those same walls shuddered from the repeated blows. Chunks of rock fell from the ceiling, narrowly missing the trio. It was a race against time to escape the relentless beast, to find a way out of the darkness that threatened to swallow them whole.

Both Isabel and Axel were also now on their feet, their

faces pale and eyes wide. Max's heart rate slowed as his mind shifted into high gear, looking for a solution, taking stock of the situation.

"Sure could use a secret escape hatch right about now," Axel grunted, his voice low and tense.

"Agreed. Go find one, okay?"

"On it," Axel said sarcastically.

Isabel was busily examining the contents of the cave, and there was much more than one might expect. Rocky apertures high up in the Himalayas did not tend to come stocked with crates and barrels, but this one appeared as well-provisioned as an old-timey general store. At least, it did until they began looking inside the crates and barrels.

"Looks like whoever was in here used up most of the goods before they left," Max said. "A real bummer, because I could really go for some hardtack right about now."

At that moment, the creature took another run at the boulder and sent the cave into another terrifying tremor.

"You think that will hold?" Axel wondered.

Max shrugged, moving on to another crate. "That depends on how long that thing keeps it up."

"Something found, I have!" Isabel shouted, her excitement sending her English into full Yoda Mode.

Max ran toward her, stumbling just a bit as the floor shook once more as the creature continued assaulting the door. Drawing up short beside her, Max stared at the piece of large equipment sitting on an overturned wooden crate.

"It's an old radio unit," he breathed.

Immediately, his mind was filled with the recording they

had heard playing from his laptop. The horrible sounds … the scream.

The other were clearly thinking the same, because Axel said,

"I guess that explains these bones."

Max and Isabel whipped around. There, on the floor, were the remains of a man. The body was remarkably well-preserved, no doubt due to the cold temperatures at this altitude, and had obviously been subject to severe trauma. The lower torso had been ripped open, while one arm and the bottom portion of the right leg had been torn off, now lying about a yard apart.

"Looks like we found where that recording originated," Max said, voicing what everyone else was almost certainly thinking. "And I think we're facing the same beast."

"How long ago was this?" Axel said. "The 1930s? That's a long-living creature."

Max shrugged and then ducked as another chuck of rock fell from above until the beast's assault. "Humans can live to be over one hundred. Tortoises can beat that. Ocean quahogs can go for hundreds of years."

"While you are talking the bullshit," Isabel said, "here is another thing I have found."

Max looked to see what she was holding, but instead she was merely pointing. As he followed her indication, his breath hitched. There, just off to the side of the radio, sat a rectangular wooden box. He jumped forward and grabbed it as Axel reached out to grip his shoulder.

"Take it easy, man. We don't know what's in there."

The creature outside again crashed into the rock, and

this time there was a sickening, crunching *crack!* as the rock began splitting down the middle. In the flash of light from a headlamp, Max just caught sight of a mass of dark fur as whatever was trying to eat them backed up for another run. The beast's enormous size and terrifying power were evident in the destruction it was causing, and a new wave of dread washed over Max.

His heart hammered in his chest, his breathing shallow and rapid. He exchanged a desperate glance with Isabel and Axel, knowing they were running out of time.

"We don't have time to take it easy," Max shot back. "That thing's going to be in here at any minute. Who's got ideas?" As he spoke, he lifted the box and gave it a cursory examination. He desperately wanted to sit down and give it a good going-over, but as Axel had so succinctly put it, there was simply no time. Even now, the creature was crashing into the rock barrier and the crack was widening with every impact.

With one trembling finger, Max pressed a small metal clasp on the front of the box. A tiny *click* sounded, and the lid popped up about a quarter-inch. Heart thudding wildly, he opened the lid the rest of the way and looked down at a tightly rolled scroll.

"Uh ... guys?"

But neither Axel nor Isabel was listening. Instead, their attention was pinned toward the entrance of the cave, where the split in the rock was now large enough to reveal the blue, glowing eyes of the creature now staring in at them. Its broad face was covered in dark fur, and as it looked inward, its broad mouth opened in a roar that shook the mountain and made Max's hair stand straight up in terror. The sound was a deafening, primal call. Its fangs gleamed in the light from their lamps, sharp and menacing. Spittle dripped from long canines, a vivid reminder of the fate that awaited them. The cave seemed to grow colder as the creature's chilling presence seeped into every cranny and crevice.

"That rock's going to go on the next attack," Axel said, his voice oddly vacant, as if he were speaking only to himself. "And then that thing will be on top of us in a moment's time."

As if acting on these words, the creature's face disappeared from view as it retreated, no doubt preparing to mount the very attack Axel had mentioned.

"And the escape hatch?" Max asked.

"Negative. I think this might be—"

Axel cut himself off and cocked his head to listen. Through the bellowing of the creature came another sound, this one less terrifying and much more familiar. All three explorers looked at each other, stunned expressions on their faces.

"Is that ... a helicopter?" Max said, disbelief coloring his voice.

Even as he spoke, Max's words were blotted out by a new rushing monster, this one made of black metal, flashing lights, and whirling blades. The chopper swooped past the mountainside with a mighty whine and roar of turbines, and Max saw the first creature stop in mid-rush to assess this new enemy. Its blue, glowing eyes tracked the red and green navigation lights of the aircraft as it streaked through the night sky.

"It's distracted," Max said, trying not to be heard by the creature but also having to yell to be heard. "This might be our chance to get out through the split in the rock!"

Going directly toward the beast did not seem a great idea, but there also did not appear to be any other way out of the cave. They were sitting ducks.

"Let's do it," Axel said, his voice steely and committed. "It's the only chance we've got."

As one, hearts pounding, the trio headed for the mouth of the cave. Max was pretty sure he and Isabel could squeeze through, but he had to push down a nagging concern about Axel's broad shoulders.

Max and Isabel slipped through the splintered boulder, their breaths held, as Axel followed closely behind. The noise of the helicopter provided a brief window of opportunity, masking the sounds of their escape. Axel's shoulders caught on the jagged edges of the rock, but with a grunt and a surge of adrenaline, he forced himself through.

And then the three emerged on the other side, gasping for air.

The creature hesitated, watching as the chopper turned, circling back around. It glanced back at the three people who were now easing their way along the mountainside, like teenager trying to sneak back into the house after missing curfew. The creature let out a deep, phlegmy *huff* and shook its massive, hairy head. It was clearly confused and uncertain. It wanted the delicious meal of Max and the others, but also could not ignore the flying contraption that was even now beginning the final part of the loop that would bring it back in line.

And then it made up its addled mind.

"It's going to charge us!" Max bellowed. "Run!"

As the creature gathered itself, the helicopter also rushing onward, flicking on a powerful, directional searchlight as it came. The searing, stabbing beam illuminated the terrifying scene as it seemed to play out in slow motion.

The creature surged forward, roaring so loudly Max thought his eardrums might burst. Then something flashed beneath the chopper, and Max's mind flew back to a previous adventure in Guatemala when he had encountered a helicopter much the same as this one.

Hellfire missile, he thought. *What the shit are they doing—they could hit us too!*

"Get down!" he screamed, pushing Isabel hard in the back to speed along her adoption of the prone position.

Then he followed suit.

He couldn't see Axel, but hoped his friend had heard him, because at that moment, the missile—for that is exactly what it was—slammed into the side of the mountain with a concussive *whump!* that turned Max's innards to jelly.

"Holy shit!" This from Isabel, who had flipped over onto her back and now stared in disbelief at the bloom of flame that flickering across the features of her slackened face.

The explosion, quite understandably, had gotten the creature's attention, and it turned back as the chopper swooped low over the ravine that dropped off not far from the cave entrance.

So that's what they were doing, Max thought. *A distraction.*

The monster reared up to its full height to confront this foe that spat fire. Its massive frame, highlighted by the spotlight, cast a huge, ominous shadow over the jagged rocks as it teetered on the lip of the ravine. With an enraged roar, the beast clawed at the airborne metal beast like King Kong fighting the biplanes, a battle of ancient instincts versus modern technology.

Max, Isabel, and Axel stared in awe and trepidation as the monstrous creature swung its powerful arms with incredible speed and ferocity. The helicopter pilot executed evasive maneuvers, weaving through the night sky in a desperate attempt to avoid the deadly grasp of the behemoth.

As Max watched, one giant fist did score a glancing blow on the right landing skid, sending a shudder through the helicopter's frame. The impact was enough to cause the craft to briefly pitch downward, and for a heart-stopping moment, it seemed as though the machine might be swallowed by the abyss below. But the pilot, maintaining nerve amidst chaos, regained control and rolled away out of reach, narrowly escaping. The monster, momentarily thwarted, let out a guttural cry that reverberated through the air.

The helicopter began another turn, possibly lining up for another try with a missile, but as the deafening sound of its engines lessened, Max became aware of a low rumbling from somewhere far up the mountain.

"Oh dear god, no," he muttered.

Isabel turned her still-stricken face toward him. "What is it?"

"You hear that?"

Both Isabel and Axel listened.

"I do," Axel said. "And if it's what I think it is, we're in deep shit."

The creature had heard the sound as well, for it had paused in its raging and now stood still, its head turned slightly to the side.

"What is it!" Isabel demanded.

Max gulped, even as the rumbling grew louder. "Avalanche," he choked out. "And I'd tell you to run, but I'm not sure where to run *to!*"

"The ravine," Axel barked. "Let's go!"

Max hesitated. "But—"

"Come on!"

And then they were all running straight for the ravine that dropped down an untold distance into frigid blackness.

As they went, Max expected the monster to intersect their route and pick them off with ease, but it seemed to understand the meaning of the sound that still grew louder above them. No doubt it had experience with avalanches and knew of their danger. It let out a roar, but this time it was less vengeful and more desperate.

On they ran, with only yards to go.

The helicopter had completed its circuit and was again preparing its pass. The powerful hum of its engines filled the air as it sliced through the darkness. As it approached, the searchlight illuminated the mountainside, casting a stark, eerie glow over the rugged terrain. Max hazarded a glance over his shoulder, curiosity and apprehension tugging at him.

He shouldn't have.

There, rushing down the mountain with unbelievable

speed, was a massive wall of snow. It roared like a freight train, obliterating everything in its path. Boulders and rocks tumbled along before it, like a tsunami pushing a fleet of fishing boats in its wake—nature's raw power on full display. Max had never seen an avalanche before, and it was one of the most terrifying things he had ever witnessed.

On they ran, the ravine's black maw stretched wide before them, the cold wind of an updraft rushing out like the freezing breath of a prehistoric Ice Age giant. The helicopter was on them, rolling slightly to complete the pass.

The creature howled.

Max spotted the slightly crumpled running skid. Reaching back, he grabbed Isabel's hand and then reached forward and grabbed Axel's.

"Ax! Jump for the skid!"

For a moment, he thought perhaps his friend had not heard him over the head-splitting roar that shook the air all around them, but then Axel seemed to crouch in mid-run. Just as they went over the edge, Axel used the lip of the ravine to propel himself up and into the open sky, reaching out with one powerful arm and hooking it around the chopper's bent skid. Then they were rushing through the air, hanging from the skid like barrel monkeys—Axel connected to the chopper, Max connected to Axel, and Isabel connected to Max.

"Hold on!" Max shouted—or tried to, but the wind snatched away his words even as they left his mouth. It was foolish anyway, for none of them had any intention of letting go.

The chopper rolled ever so slightly, and Max watched

with horrified fascination as the avalanche stampeded down the mountain and gushed into the ravine.

Where the cave had been—where the monster had stood—was now nothing more than a solid blanket of white, as if it had all been nothing more than a pencil drawing and the avalanche had been the eraser.

24

"ALL THE CHANG YOU CAN DRINK!" DOG ANNOUNCED, WALKING out of the kitchen with his arms full of cans. He set them down in the middle of the long dining table and everyone gathered around, helping themselves.

"What's this stuff again?" asked the helicopter pilot, McGreavy. Without waiting for an answer, he popped the top and guzzled a healthy portion. "Actually, never mind. When it tastes this good, I don't care what it is."

Max swiped a can for himself and then settled down on the bench. He was unspeakably worn out. The physical exertion plus the high-octane events had drained him. He wanted only to drink this can of chang and then lie down on a cot in which no one had died.

But Axel had questions.

"So you were sent out here by the Prof?" he asked McGreavy.

The pilot was now flanked by two official looking men

who had apparently been aboard the helicopter as well. Max recognized them as Dunder and Simmons, from the supersecret agency with which Professor Barnes was somehow involved. Both agents had played a role in Max's prior adventure in Guatemala, and he was still uncertain exactly how he felt about them.

"We'll handle the Q&A," Dunder said, taking charge. He sat down near Max, opened his can, and sipped at it almost daintily. "When you contacted your father over the satellite radio, it raised a lot of questions. Not the least of which was why the hell were you even here. And when the call was suddenly ended, and we were unable to reach you afterwards, well ... we decided we should pay a little visit. Something was clearly up."

"And given this can be a touchy part of the world," Simmons cut in, "we figured the sooner the better. Plus, for some reason, Professor Barnes still cares about all of you." He rolled his eyes. "Can't figure out why. Nothing but trouble, from my way of thinking."

"Your way of thinking is disturbing," Max said, "but I'm glad you showed up. We were about to become a midnight snack for what I can only assume was the Migoi."

"Oh, speaking of that sonofabitch!" Kane roared, coming to his feet. "It's time for a moment of silence. That asshole broke ol' Fitch right in half on its way to get you people, so let's give that guy his due."

Without hesitation, all conversation ceased and everyone stood or sat quietly. From somewhere, Max heard a muttered prayer. A few moments later, Kane roared again,

"To Fitch!"

He drained his can of beer.

"To Fitch!" they all echoed, following suit.

And then everything went back to normal.

"Yeah, that's something I don't need to see ever again," Dunder said. "When we landed at the camp to let you three loons off the skid, I couldn't believe my eyes. That poor guy had been snapped like a twig."

At the mention of the skid, Max instinctively flexed his fingers. He had lost all feeling in that hand before the chopper had finally landed, and the three explorers had to be nearly pried apart.

"And I think that's what it wanted to do to us," Max said. "So again, thank you." He glanced at McGreavy. "I see your ability with the Hellfire has not improved."

"Okay, so I missed the ... whatever it was," the pilot groaned. Then he raised one finger to clarify. "But I wasn't drunk this time. This time I was just incompetent."

They all laughed, remembering McGreavy's horrific display of marksmanship in Central America.

"Back to my questions, though," Axel said once the mirth had subsided.

Dunder raised a forestalling hand. "You're going to have to talk with Professor Barnes. We were sent to check on you and get you out if necessary. Anything beyond that is a closed book, as far as you are concerned."

"I'm starting to remember why I found you annoying," Max grunted. "I might need more chang to forget again."

Dunder allowed himself a brief smile and rolled a can toward the archaeologist, who accepted it gratefully.

Max had not expected to get much from the agents, and

he was more eager to speak with his father anyway. Hopefully, the agents could expedite their departure from Tibet to avoid the bumpy ride back to Lhasa and the flight to Shanghai. Certainly, many questions remained to be answered, not the least of which was exactly what was going on in the basecamp and how much his father knew about. But, again, that would have to wait for now.

Max felt in his parka with one hand and smiled into his can of beer as he pressed against the rough surface of the wooden box.

At least we found the scroll, he thought. *This wasn't a complete waste.*

Did you, though? Paranoia chirped. *Could it really be that easy?*

Max's beer smile changed to a frown. *Look, not everything has to be insanely challenging. Maybe we just got lucky this time.*

Paranoia snickered. *Sure, sure. Believe whatever you want.*

"Thanks," Max said. "I will."

"What you will do, Max?" Isabel asked, lightly touching his arm.

"Huh? Oh, nothing."

"It is the voice?"

Max grimaced, feeling embarrassed. "Maybe."

And it was then he realized that the moment Isabel had touched him, Paranoia had quieted.

Interesting, he thought. *Very interesting, indeed.*

Pushing back from the table, he set down the newly empty can and stood up, stretching.

"If you'll all excuse me, I need to become unconscious for a while. Where can I crash?"

"Take Fitch's," Kane called out. "Not to be unfeeling, but he won't be needing it."

"To Fitch!" Grits yelled.

"To Fitch!" everyone echoed.

Max participated in the verbal salute and then walked from the community building into the crisp morning air. The sun was just coming up, turning the white-capped mountains into the most flawless of diamonds. Tibet was a strange, mysterious, and wonderful place. He would miss it, even with all the dangers encountered within its borders, and hoped that one day he would be able to return under different circumstances.

Then he chuckled and headed toward Fitch's tent.

"Who are you kidding, Barnes?" he muttered. "You'll never change. If you weren't almost getting killed, you'd be bored witless. Now shut up and go get some sleep. Sure, it's another dead man's cot, but at least he didn't die *in* the cot."

Max found the tent, crawled inside, and collapsed onto the cot. He half-expected the macabre circumstances to cause him trouble, but almost immediately he began drifting into the poppy fields of early slumber, secure in the knowledge that he and his friends were safe—at least for now. His hand gripped the rough exterior of the scroll's box, as somewhere overhead, a Himalayan golden eagle sent out its cry.

THE END

A NOTE ABOUT REVIEWS

If you enjoyed this book, a review would mean the world. Reviews are so important to authors and are essential to being able to market books effectively.

Just a line or two makes a huge difference!

Thank you!

ABOUT THE AUTHOR

Craig A. Hart is the stay-at-home father of twin boys, an author, and audiobook narrator. A native of Grand Rapids, Michigan, Craig lives in Iowa City, Iowa with his wife, sons, insane dog, and anti-social cat.

He is the author of the Shelby Alexander Thriller Series, the historical mystery *Night at Key West,* and co-author of the Maxwell Barnes Adventure Thriller series.

For up-to-date info on new releases, follow Craig on BookBub at: bookbub.com/profile/craig-a-hart